Something
Brides of Cedar Bend
Old

LENA HART

ISBN-13: 978-1-941885-27-7

Books by Lena Hart

To the lovely and brilliant ladies of the Destin Retreat for helping me plot through "The End" of this story.

Big thanks to Kianna Alexander and Kaia Danielle for that much needed "aha!" moment.

And hugs and kisses to Farrah Rochon for making that retreat happen!

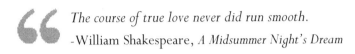 *The course of true love never did run smooth.*
-William Shakespeare, *A Midsummer Night's Dream*

Prologue

Cedar Bend, Virginia

WHAT AM I DOING?

I can't do this.

Not that she didn't want to be with him—she loved him with everything she had—but she just couldn't start the kind of life he wanted.

Not right now, anyway.

Mya slowly rose from the bed and wrapped the single sheet around her breasts. She glanced back to see if Guy would wake.

He didn't.

With a small sigh of relief, she slid out of the large bed and quickly navigated her way out of the room and into the connecting bathroom. This was her first night sleeping with Guy, and she didn't know if he was a light sleeper or not. She kept her movements slow, not wanting to chance it if he was.

With the bed sheet wrapped around her, she sat on the lid of the toilet and dropped her head on her hands.

What's the matter with me?

She had just buried her father barely a week ago and now she was here starting a new life with Guy? Forgetting all about her old life, her home—a home that had been made up of just her and her dad for the last fifteen years.

"Oh, Daddy. You were right."

A wave of grief assailed her and the tears began to pour out. They clouded her vision then fell, scalding a path down her cheeks. She covered her mouth, muffling her cries. She loved Guy and could never forget tonight, but a part of her wasn't ready to start a new life with him.

Not yet.

But if she told him how she felt about everything, he would just say that it was her grief talking. Maybe it was, but she couldn't stifle the panic that was rising in her.

Burying her face into her hands, Mya let the rest of her grief erupt from her while she struggled internally with her decision.

Guy had been unbelievably supportive these past few weeks during the preparation for her father's funeral, but she couldn't accept moving in with him—much less jumping into this new life he seemed determined to start.

Things are moving too fast.

Keeping the bed sheet wrapped closely around her, Mya sprang to her feet and slipped quietly out of the bathroom. Her clothes were littered at the foot of the bed and she snatched them up.

She stole a quick glance at Guy's still form, but he remained sleeping deeply on his stomach, an arm tucked beneath the pillow.

For a brief moment, indecision kept her frozen where she stood. A part of her wanted to crawl back into bed and have him hold her again, yet another equally strong desire compelled her to get far away from him and back to the comfort of her own home.

For most of her life, she had let her father take care of her, had depended on his presence and protection for so long. He had been a constant in her life and now he was gone...

And Guy was trying to take his place.

She couldn't let that happen.

Tearing her gaze from his sleeping form, Mya quickly grabbed her dress and snuck out of the bedroom. She didn't want to hurt him, but she couldn't face him either.

Fully dressed, Mya searched for her boots, trying her best to make as little noise as possible. She carefully maneuvered her way through the dark ranch-style home until she found them by the door. She decided to carry them outside, grateful her purse and keys were where she'd left them—in her car.

It was a bad habit she needed to break, but having a sheriff for a father—and a deputy for a boyfriend—had spoiled her.

Mya carefully unhooked her jacket from the wall and slipped out of the house. The air was chilly, despite summer fast approaching, and she tugged on her denim jacket. Letting the moonlight guide her steps, she rushed to her car and started the ignition.

For a moment, she sat there, staring out at the dark house. He would never forgive her for this, and she balked at the thought of him hating her.

A flash of panic seized her and she shut her eyes at the indecision that still tore her apart.

What am I doing?

Am I really going to leave him alone in bed tonight?

Tonight of all nights?

Mya opened her eyes and once again peered up at his house. Instead of seeing a home where she would spend the rest of her life with the man she loved, she saw a dark, ominous structure that looked more like a prison. An intense feeling of confinement overcame her and she knew what she needed to do.

Too much had changed in such a short time. She needed to get away, to be on her own.

She needed time to think.

Mya searched around her car for a notepad. As she began to write, slight tremors shook her hand and she tightened her grip on the pen. Guy would be upset with her, but hopefully she could make him understand with her disjointed words that she did love him…

She just wasn't ready to start a new life with him.

Not yet…

Guy jerked awake at the sound of tires driving over gravel.

Who could be coming to his house at this hour?

He turned to the other side of the bed and ran his hand over the spot Mya slept on.

It was empty. And barely warm. She hadn't been gone long, but she was gone.

Where is she?

When he realized the car approaching was actually pulling away from the house, he jumped out of bed.

"Mya?"

Guy pulled on his boxers and made his way to the bathroom. Empty. Alarmed, he made his way through the quiet, dark house.

"Mya!"

This time, his shout echoed through the room and a sinking sensation began to settle in his gut. It wasn't until he found the bed sheet lying in a crumpled heap on the living room floor that the bottom of his stomach dropped.

She'd left?

Guy refused to believe that. He dialed Mya's cell phone as he quickly dressed, but each time the call went immediately to voicemail. He cursed and tossed the phone on the bed. He couldn't accept that she had walked out on him—on them. They had made a commitment to each other and he wasn't going to just let her walk out of it.

He loved her too much.

Guy finished dressing and rushed outside. If he hurried, he could probably meet her right as she was pulling into her father's home. And he knew that was where she would be. The pain of losing her father was plain for anyone to see. It had been stark on her face.

The tragic death of Sheriff Marvin Daniels had been hard for everyone in their small, close-knit town, especially the men who had served under him. For Guy, Marvin had been more than just his boss, and dealing with his death had been difficult.

But Guy had tried to hide his own grief so he could take care of the woman he loved—so he could be there for her.

And she had left him?

He jumped into his truck and cranked the engine. Maybe he had moved too fast by bringing her here. Now she was in a panic. Once he talked to her and assured her that everything was going to work out, she would see that this was the right move for them.

It wasn't until he flipped on the headlights that he saw it—a small, single sheet of paper peeking out of the windshield wipers. At first, Guy almost ignored it, but his instincts convinced him to get out of the truck.

With a vicious curse, he threw the truck back into park and jumped out. Uneasiness crawled up his spine as he wrenched the thin scrap of paper from between the rubber blades of the wipers.

Leaning against the hood of the car, Guy skimmed the letter, immediately recognizing Mya's handwriting. But it took a careful read through the second time for him to truly process what he was reading...

Guy, I'm so sorry. You know how much I love you, how long I've been in love with you, but I'm not ready for this kind of commitment right now. Everything is moving too fast and I need time to sort it all out. I need time to sort ME out. Please don't hate me.

I love you.

-Mya

Still reeling, Guy stared at the note a moment longer before he crushed it in his fist. She couldn't do what?

Be with him?

Bitter anger rose in his gut, but he tried to suppress it. So, her solution had been to leave him without the courtesy of telling him to his face. Or, at the very least, have the decency to leave the damn note in his house.

What the hell is the matter with her?

Mya had always been impulsive, a trait he had occasionally found charming, but there was nothing appealing about being left in bed alone by the woman he had planned to spend the rest of his life with.

Had tonight meant nothing to her?

He'd spent these past few years building a fantasy in his head of the two of them filling this house with children and living happily ever after. But that was what it had been. A fantasy.

Guy pushed away from his truck and headed back inside. He realized he still held the crushed letter in his hand, and his grip tightened until it was a ball of scrap paper. He'd been a damn fool, offering his heart and home, thinking they could make a future together when obviously that hadn't been what she wanted.

He found the rumpled bed sheet on the floor and grabbed it. It still held her scent. He could make out the faint toasted, honey-like fragrance that came from her homemade soaps yet was unique to her. He loved the warm, light aroma. It always reminded him of her.

Tossing the sheet aside, Guy marched into the bedroom and stripped the bedding. Her smell was everywhere and he couldn't stand it.

He should have seen this coming, should have anticipated it. His problem was that he thought he'd understood her—thought a life with him was what she wanted.

How wrong he'd been.

For as long as he'd known Mya, she had been flighty. It was her nature. Not to mention their nine-year age gap. At thirty, he was ready to settle down, to start a family of his own. He'd made the mistake of thinking she, at twenty-one, would want the same thing. When all was said and done, it shouldn't have come as a surprise that her feelings for him would also be fickle.

And yet it did.

His only thought these past few days had been to make her happy again, but just because his happiness centered around her, didn't mean she felt that way about him.

It was clear to him now that she didn't feel for him what he did for her, and whatever it was she wanted, she hadn't found it in him.

He'd been an idiot to think he could make her happy, and an even bigger fool to think they could actually have a future together. They had never been right for each other and he should have recognized that from the start.

Tonight had been a mistake.

One he would never make again.

One

Two years later…

"THREE THOUSAND, right?"

"Yup. Three grand and she's all yours."

Mya Daniels turned away from the man who went only by "Bob" and went to study the car again.

The man was an older gentleman, though she couldn't make out his true age with the baseball cap covering his pale brown face. But she could make out his hazel eyes, and they were gentle eyes—the kind that didn't make her reluctant to hand over what was left of her savings for the used Jeep Wrangler.

They had arranged to meet at the parking lot of the motel she'd checked into near the airport. She hadn't bothered to rent a car when she'd arrived in Virginia last night and could only hope she was making a good purchase.

Not that she had much of a choice.

She needed a car, and it was the only thing she could afford within her current budget. As long as it got her home, she didn't particularly care about the faint clunking noise that had come from under the hood when

Bob had pulled up. And she also wouldn't have to trouble Gloria to make the near two-hour drive to pick her up.

The thought of Guy's mother brought up memories of him, and a wave of emotion washed over her. The same kind of heated fluster that always came over her when she thought about him. She couldn't deny that he was the main reason why she was returning back to Cedar Bend, yet she didn't know what exactly she was returning to. In the two years she'd been away, they had not once talked. He simply refused to speak to her.

Well, she was home now—or at least she would be, once she got herself on the road—and there would be no avoiding her.

Mya took one last look at the car and made her way back to Bob. Overall, it seemed to be in working condition and just as Bob had advertised. She handed him the cashier's check, which he instantly pocketed, and he handed her the keys, along with the car title. It was all done.

Her first big purchase.

"So we're all set?"

He nodded. "I just have to grab one thing and you can be on your way."

Mya watched as he pulled out a screwdriver from his back pocket and began to fiddle with the license plate on the back of the car.

"What are you doing?"

"Taking my plates, honey." He looked up at her. "Don't you have any?"

She shook her head. Why would she randomly have a set of car plates with her? But then again, Bob didn't know that she had just flown back from her two-year visit to England. Nor did he know that this was her first time owning anything this significant, much less a car.

"Well, you can't be on the road without plates."

"Where can I buy them, then?"

He chuckled. "It doesn't work like that, little darling." He laughed again, shaking his head. "Let me see what I can find."

He went back into the truck and rummaged through the front dashboard. Within seconds, he came back to where she stood, carrying another document.

"Now, this will probably get you to where you're going until you can register for some new ones."

Mya watched as Bob placed the temporary plates on the back of her car. After a few minutes, he straightened.

"Try not to get yourself pulled over." With the tip of his baseball cap, he turned and left.

"Gee, thanks," Mya muttered after him.

It took her only a half-hour after that to pile her suitcases into the car, check out of her motel room, and get on the freeway. She was finally heading home...

To Guy.

A nervous laugh burst out of her. Not many would have traded the exciting life of living in Europe for a small mountain town like Cedar Bend, but she had.

Cedar Bend was her home. She realized that now. And she missed it—missed the way it smelled after the rain, missed the way the flowers bloomed over the boardwalk of Promise Lane. She missed the quiet sounds, the warm people.

She missed Guy.

Behind the wheel of her black and red Wrangler, Mya sped down the highway, eager to get back home to her old friends and fam—

Her hands involuntarily tightened around the steering wheel. No, she didn't have any family at Cedar Bend. Not really. Unless she counted Guy. He was her family now.

He had always been.

Two years of running away with her heart locked in a box hadn't helped her any. Nothing or no one had been able to replace what she'd lost…or what she had left behind.

Her mother's invitation to spend some time with her and her new family had seemed to Mya like a good idea at the time. But the longer she'd stayed, the more Mya realized she had only been running away from her pain. Leaving the country hadn't eased the heartache of losing her dad. It had only made things worse, because she had lost Guy too.

No, I haven't.

She couldn't accept that. It may have taken her two years to understand what she had given up, but now that she did, she wanted to make things right. She wanted her man back.

But does he still want me?

Mya ignored the aggravating question that had plagued her since she had decided to leave her mother's home in London and return to her old life in Virginia. Yet the closer she got to Cedar Bend, the more incessant the question became.

She sighed. Guy had loved her once, and as much as she believed nothing could come between them, she couldn't be sure if he would be happy to see her. He had spent the past two years refusing to speak to her, despite her many attempts, and the sting of his rebuff was searing.

Walking out on him that night hadn't been the right move. She knew that now. He was as proud as he was loving. But she knew him. And she knew, no matter what, he wouldn't break their promise to each other.

He just wouldn't.

Mya pushed the disheartening thoughts aside. The welcome sign into Cedar Bend came into view ahead. Her heart began to beat in a quick tempo of excitement and anticipation. It wouldn't be long now before she saw him again. Face to face.

She debated whether she should go straight to her father's home or just head over to Guy's place. Would he even be home? It was late in the afternoon. He could still be at the station.

It was probably best she freshen up first, anyway. Maybe change into something nice before she saw him. It also wouldn't hurt for her to do something with her unruly curls…

Completely absorbed in her thoughts, Mya didn't realize how fast she was going until it was too late. Red and blue lights flashed behind her just before the sirens sounded.

She groaned. "Oh, come on."

Following procedure, she reduced her speed and pulled over to the shoulder of the road. She rolled down the window and waited as the officer approached her car.

"Ma'am, do you know why I stopped you?"

Mya studied the officer's face, which was partly shielded by his wide-brim hat, hoping it would be someone she recognized—or someone who recognized her. But there was nothing familiar about this officer. Her father had been sheriff of Cedar Bend for as long as she could remember, and she was pretty familiar with many of the men on the force. Though, since she'd been gone for two years, she couldn't make that claim anymore.

"I know I may have been going a little fast, Officer…" She glanced at his name badge. Deputy-Officer Michael Justice. *Really?* She almost chuckled at the appropriateness of his name.

"Ma'am, you were going eighty-five in a forty-five."

Mya bit her lower lip. She had never gotten a citation before, but from the no-nonsense look of the officer, there was a slim chance she would be getting out of this ticket. It didn't hurt to try though…

"Sorry, officer. I didn't realize I was going so fast. If you could just let me off with a warning, I'll be sure to watch my speed next time."

The deputy cocked a brow, clearly unmoved by her apology. "I'm going to need to see your license and registration."

She rummaged in her large tote, grateful her mustard-yellow wallet wasn't buried in the bottom of the bag. She managed to force a smile to her lips when she handed him the card.

"I just bought this car not too long ago, and I don't have the registration yet."

The deputy peered down at her license and inspected it with such scrutiny, she cringed again. She could imagine what he might be thinking looking down at the three-year-old picture. Her cheeks had been rounder from a bad allergy season, and that year she had decided to chop off her hair to the root, getting rid of the damaged ends caused by her hair relaxer. Needless to say, it hadn't been her best picture moment. Her face, however, had since slimmed down, and her thick, curly hair now hung around her neck.

"You're a resident of Cedar Bend?"

Mya nodded, relieved her home address was recognizable to him. She caught his curious glance at the piles of luggage stuffed in her back seat.

"I've been travelling and just got back into town today," she explained.

"When did you purchase the vehicle?"

"This morning."

"Then I'll need to see the title."

Mya fished through her purse for the papers, not quite sure why her heart was racing. It beat against her chest so loudly, she wouldn't be surprised if the deputy could hear it.

This is just a routine stop.

She wouldn't let news of the recent tension between the police and community turn her into a nervous wreck. News of the violence around the country while she'd been overseas had been disheartening to hear, but her father had been sheriff of this town. He had trained many of Cedar Bend's officers. If he had trusted them, then so would she.

Mya handed the deputy the paperwork and watched as he carefully examined it.

"I paid cash for it."

She didn't know what purpose that useless information served, but she could only hope the officer wouldn't ask her about the temporary tags attached to the back of the car.

"Wait right here."

Her grip tightened on the wheel. *Great.* From her rearview mirror, she watched as Officer Justice got back into his cruiser. Several long minutes passed before the officer returned to the side of her vehicle. From his stern expression, she could tell there was trouble.

"Ms. Daniels, I'm going to need you to step out of the vehicle."

Her heart sank. "May I ask why?"

"Those tags aren't registered to this vehicle, and they're also expired. There's no record of this vehicle so I'm going to have to impound it."

"What?"

"I'm sure we can get this all straightened out down at the station, but I'm going to need you to step calmly out of the car."

"Am I being arrested?"

"No, not yet."

Not yet?

The words hadn't fully processed as she reluctantly opened the door and stepped out into the cool February weather. A faint buzzing began ringing in her ears and she shivered, not sure if it was from anxiety or the gust of wind that blew over her.

This could not be happening. Not now.

Her first day back home should be spent reuniting with her old friends, not at the police station where her father's men would watch and wonder—where Guy would wonder...

At the thought of him, hope coursed through her.

"Officer, please. This is all a big mistake. Just let me call Guy Lawson and he'll straighten this all out."

The officer paused. "Sheriff Lawson?"

So he really was the town's new sheriff?

Gloria had mentioned it before during one of their calls, but Mya tried to avoid any discussions about Guy. The less they spoke about him, the less homesick Mya felt at the end of their talks.

"Yes, he knows me. He's—" She stopped before she said too much. That was one card she wasn't going to play. Only they knew what they were to each other. "Please, just call him. I didn't steal this car. I'm not a thief! He can tell you that."

"I didn't say you were, Ms. Daniels. But right now, I need to take you down to the station. You can speak to the sheriff then and get this all straightened out."

Mya slowly shook her head. To have Guy and everyone at the station see her returning to town like some criminal was humiliating. "You need to call him now. He won't be happy with you detaining me like this."

Officer Justice hesitated for a moment, eyeing her warily. Mya took advantage of his apparent indecision.

"Please." Desperation made her words come out more forcefully than she intended. *"Just call him."*

"Don't leave this spot," he ordered then headed back to his cruiser.

Mya leaned against the old—possibly stolen—car and released a long sigh of relief. She knew she was taking a gamble. After two years, she couldn't be sure how Guy would react to finding out that she was back in Cedar Bend. But there was one thing she was certain about—Guy would save her.

He always had.

Two

IF HE DIDN'T LOVE his job, he would have walked out of the pretentious mayor's office right then.

But Guy Lawson did love his job.

He loved his town and he cared about the men who worked to serve and protect it alongside him. It would have been the ultimate insult to walk away from it now. That, he couldn't do. Not when the man Guy so respected had worked his ass off to create a unit the good people of Cedar Bend could trust.

Summoning all the patience he had cultivated over the years as an officer of the law, Guy sat across the mayor and listened as the pompous man proceeded to leverage his promotion for a political endorsement.

"Now Guy, you know how much I appreciate your hard work these past couple of years, but it's an election year and every decision I make will be scrutinized and judged."

"I don't believe appointing me sheriff will affect your campaign, Warren. Last I checked, there haven't been any complaints about me or my men."

"You are sheriff, Guy."

"I'm interim sheriff, which basically makes me a placeholder until someone else is put into the position. And the way I see it, I've more than proved myself."

"You're absolutely right. In proving yourself, I mean. I'm not taking that away from you, but you have to understand there are budget restraints."

Bullshit.

Guy, however, clenched his jaw to keep the curse from spewing out. "I'm already doing the work without the pay, Warren. We've already lost a few good men because of the cuts. What more do you want?"

Mayor Warren Powers sat back in his leather executive chair and regarded Guy with sharp brown eyes that revealed little of his thoughts.

"Guy, I'm well aware of your value to this town. The people here love you and you've done a great job heading up the department. In fact, I know that making your position as sheriff permanent could only help my campaign. But I hope you can appreciate the awkward position that places me in."

"What are you saying?"

"Well, if I appointed you sheriff now, then it would look as if I'm offering favors for an endorsement. But if you were to announce who you are lending your support toward before, well then…that would change things."

Guy tensed. In other words, Powers wanted his endorsement. Obviously, the good mayor wouldn't come right out and say it, but Guy knew when he was being played. He also knew he had substantial influence in the town.

If he lent his support to Warren Powers, Guy would be securing his own promotion while helping the current mayor rise back up in the polls. Maybe even win a third term in office, which was not something many people of Cedar Bend were inclined to see happen.

Guy couldn't blame them. They were frustrated by the mayor's lack of action on issues impacting the community and angry at the man's autocratic stance on unpopular policies.

"I understand this is an awkward time for you, what with Benson running against me, but I trust you'll put your friendship aside and consider your career. I could certainly use your support for this run."

There it was. Nothing like a good old-fashioned, underhanded threat to piss him off.

Guy could put up with a lot from the mayor. Hell, he'd already suffered enough of the man's bullshit these past two years. But he wouldn't tolerate anyone, not even his "boss," manipulating him.

"Are you threatening my job?" Under Guy's steady gaze, the mayor shifted in his seat.

"Don't be ridiculous," Warren scoffed, then released a nervous chuckle. "You need to lighten up, son. You take things too seriously. I only meant you shouldn't let old friendships get in the way of you making new partnerships."

"I don't."

"I'm glad to hear that. This election is gearing up to be an intense one. Together, however, I think we will make a great team. I believe, with you in my corner, we can win this thing."

Guy doubted both of those assumptions. Right now, Warren Powers was far below where he needed to be in the polls. It would probably take more than an endorsement to change that.

Between Warren Powers and his good friend Eric Benson, Guy couldn't say for certain just yet who the right man for the position was. But if he had to choose based on track record, he wouldn't cast his vote for Warren. The man was a glutton for power with little regard to the citizens of Cedar Bend. Maybe the town could use a fresh mind like Eric's in office. He was smart, sharp, and more vested in their small town in a way that Powers wasn't.

And what Warren lacked in integrity, Eric had in abundance.

"Look, Warren, I haven't made a decision on a candidate as of yet. Right now, my main concern is boosting morale at the station and getting more officers back in the unit."

Besides, Guy cared too much about the people at Cedar Bend not to take their issues into account. He wouldn't trade in their trust in him for a promotion, no matter how much he wanted it.

The mayor was silent for a moment then nodded. "I absolutely agree. We need to build back confidence and prove to the people of Cedar Bend that we are working for them."

"Can we discuss a new budget for the department, then? We have an immediate need for another full-time deputy."

The mayor rose from his seat. "In due time, Sheriff Lawson, in due time. For now, let's just work on strengthening our partnership."

Guy ground his teeth together and pushed himself to his feet. Just more stalling and game-playing, he was sure, but that didn't stop him from taking the mayor's outstretched hand. Guy would play his game and keep him guessing, until he could get his department fully staffed again.

"By the way, Guy, will you be free next weekend?"

Guy stopped at the door. "I'm not sure yet. Why?"

"I'm having a dinner party next Friday night, a formal engagement, and I would love for you to be there."

At his unexpected invitation, Guy could only stare blankly at the mayor. In the two years he'd been in this position, the mayor had never invited him over to his home, or any formal function that would require a suit jacket.

"Think about it," Warren added when Guy didn't immediately respond. "It would be good for you to personally meet and network with other members of the council." He paused then added, "Sophie will also be in attendance and could certainly use an escort."

At the mention of the man's youngest daughter, Guy stifled a groan. He didn't understand the mayor's recent fixation with trying to set the two of them up, but his matchmaking endeavors were now becoming downright blatant. Guy was certain this was just another of the mayor's conniving moves to wrangle a statement of support from him.

Evidently, Powers couldn't see that the chances of him lending his support were swiftly spiraling down to nothing.

"I'll think about it."

With those noncommittal words, Guy left the mayor's office and made his way out of the small council building, relieved to finally be out of there.

What a waste of an afternoon.

He hated this part of his job—the dance he had to do with those who sat in office just to get things accomplished in his department. When it came to politics, Guy paid attention to all facets, including the candidate's actions, not just what they had to say on certain policies. He evaluated them based on how their views would impact their small town and the nearly four thousand people who called it home. Whoever Guy decided to rally behind had to share that same interest.

Guy climbed into his service vehicle, the word *Sheriff* printed boldly on its side. There was an immense sense of pride and honor that came with the position—along with a shitload of work.

Part of him sometimes wished he hadn't taken the damn position. Then he wouldn't be forced to put up with Warren Powers or have spent the past two years being strung along by the man.

Then again, Guy couldn't let the position fall into the wrong hands. His mentor, Marvin Daniels, had worked too hard to build a police department their town could be proud of—that *he* could be proud to work for—and Guy would honor his memory by making sure he kept it intact.

He pulled into the streets, his thoughts filling with memories of the man who had been more of a father to him than his own absent one. He missed Marvin every day and wished things could have been different. Then maybe things between him and Mya would have ended differently...

The police radio crackled, jerking Guy out of his brooding thoughts.

"Hey, Guy. Do you copy?"

He sighed, recognizing his cousin over the radio. Mike still had some learning to do, but his cousin was new to his role as deputy, and therefore required a lot of patience.

"Yeah. Go ahead."

"I have a woman here that I pulled over for speeding. But turns out she's driving a car with no plates, no registration, and an expired tag."

"You should know what to do, Mike. Bring her down to the station and have Damian impound the car."

"I was getting ready to do that, but she's claiming she knows you. Said you'd be pissed if I took her in."

"Believe me, I won't be. Just do your job."

"Um, are you sure? She's from out of town, I think, though her address is listed here. She said she just got back into town today and that you would clear this all up."

Guy frowned. He didn't know any woman from out of town. None that would be so bold as to ask for him, anyway. Except...

His hand tightened around the wheel. "What's her name?"

"Zamya Daniels. According to her license."

Guy's heart lurched.

Mya?

She was back.

His heart began to race, and he was annoyed by the unwanted reaction. She had no right to it. He should have forgotten her the same way she had him when she'd left that night. The familiar anger curled in his gut as the memories flooded him. Only it hadn't been her sneaking out that had him riled. The fact that she'd left town without so much as a fucking phone call still had the power to infuriate him beyond words.

Now she was back.

And she was asking for him?

"Guy?"

He pushed his maddening thoughts aside. He had a vice-grip on the steering wheel and forced himself to relax.

"Yeah, I know her."

There was a short hesitation before Mike spoke again. "How do you want to handle it?"

Guy scoffed at the question—the same question he had asked himself these past two years. From the moment he'd found out where she fled to, he'd been torn between travelling to England and dragging her back to where she belonged. Or giving her what she evidently wanted and maintaining the distance she'd put between them.

In the end, he'd chosen the latter and had kept her at arm's length.

Now she was back.

"Bring her down to the station and put her in one of the cells. Just don't book her," Guy added. "I'm on my way there now."

"Okay, but I don't think she's going to be at all happy about that."

"Just do your job." Guy instantly regretted his harsh words.

There was a long pause before Mike spoke again. "Look, Guy, I don't want to get into your business, but…who is she?"

Guy hesitated, not sure how much he should tell his cousin. In the end, it didn't matter much. She was back now, and that could only mean she was finally going to put an end to it.

"She's my wife."

Three

GUY STRODE into the police station, aware of the eyes following his every move. Mike may be new to town and unfamiliar with his relationship with Mya, but the other deputies weren't as oblivious. They knew just how serious he'd been about Sheriff Daniels' daughter and had been just as curious about her departure. Like everyone else in town.

Ignoring the looks, Guy headed straight to Mike's desk. "Take me to her."

Mike got to his feet and they made their way down the long corridor to the holding cells.

"Has she said anything?"

"Nope. She's been real quiet since I brought her in." Mike blew out a frustrated breath. "Damn it, Guy. You should have told me who she really was."

"I did."

"I mean about her being Sheriff Daniels' daughter."

Guy scoffed. *Of course.* Being the former sheriff's daughter trumped being his wife. Then again, no one knew about their secret union, and until they could get their pretense of a marriage annulled, that was how it would have to stay.

A secret.

"The other guys have been giving me shit for bringing her in like this."

Guy's brows drew together. "You were doing your job," he said, annoyed by the guilt slinking through him.

Maybe he shouldn't have had Mike take her to a cell, but if she thought she would get special treatment just because she was back in town, she had sorely underestimated how angry he still was.

"What were you able to find out about the car?"

"Not much yet. I'm still waiting for a call back from the guy who sold her the thing. So far the name on the title comes back clean. She already apologized for taking the car on the road without the proper tags. She was just in a rush to get back home. Maybe you could cut her some slack."

"You've met her all of five minutes and already you're coming to her defense?"

Mike shrugged. "What can I say...I have a soft spot for a pretty face?"

Guy's frown deepened and Mike cleared his throat. They reached the second entrance to the cell units and stopped.

Before Guy could punch in the code, Mike handed him a small ring of keys.

"You're going to need this."

Guy cursed and snatched the keys from Mike's hand. "You handcuffed her?"

"You told me to bring her in."

"I also told you she was my wife." Guy may have wanted to put a scare in her, but not like this. She was his wife, after all, and though it may not mean anything to her, it meant something to him. Hell, if he was honest with himself, he would admit that it still did. "You didn't need to cuff her."

"Sorry. I'll know for next time."

"There won't be a next," he muttered.

Mike threw his hands up. "Okay. But seriously, Guy. You have to explain this one to me. When in the hell did you find time to marry and why wasn't I invited?"

"Don't worry, you didn't miss anything. This just happened."

"No. A one-night stand happens. A baby happens. A marriage…that just doesn't *happen*." Mike studied him curiously. "You mean you two eloped?"

"Something like that," Guy snapped.

Actually, it had been exactly like that, but at the time it hadn't felt like a quickie marriage. For him, he had been getting the woman he'd always wanted, and by making Mya his wife, Guy believed he could protect and take care of her the way he had promised Marvin he would.

But the harsh reality was that he hadn't married a woman. He had married a girl who hadn't been ready for the kind of commitment he was.

"Does Aunt Gloria know about this?"

Guy froze. He hadn't thought that far ahead, and blurting the truth to his cousin probably wasn't the right move. His mother would kill him for keeping such a secret from her this long. Yet she would undoubtedly be thrilled. She adored Mya.

"Ma doesn't know, and right now I'd like to keep it that way." He didn't know what was going to happen between him and Mya and didn't want his mother getting her hopes crushed. In fact, he didn't want anyone knowing just how close he and Mya really were. "I would appreciate it if you kept this quiet."

"My lips are sealed."

Guy nodded, trusting his cousin to keep his word.

He made his way down the end of the corridor, his chest constricting with the anticipation of seeing her again. He hadn't laid eyes on her or heard her voice in two years. Just when he thought he'd gotten his emotions under control where she was concerned, all the mixed feelings came roaring back to the surface.

Guy decided to welcome them, giving himself permission to feel the frustration, the anger, the suppressed desire he'd tried to contain for so long. Maybe then, when he saw her again, he would feel what he needed to feel and finally be free of this hold she had on him.

Mya stared blankly at the bleak gray wall in front of her. This was not how she envisioned her homecoming.

She couldn't believe she was actually sitting in a jail cell. Unfortunately, she had the hard concrete cot where she sat to remind her that she was right where Guy wanted her to be. She knew this was his doing. There had been some sympathy on the deputy's face when he'd placed the handcuffs around her wrists and ushered her to the police car.

She had suffered through more pity when he'd brought her to the police station and led her to the holding cell, past the other deputies. Her face still burned with mortification from that moment.

Mya rested her bound hands on her lap, clasping and unclasping them, forcing herself to relax. The metal handcuffs jingled around her wrists, serving as a cold reminder that her nightmare was still very much a reality.

Heavy footsteps echoed down the hall and drew near. Her heart pounded in rapid tempo, and she knew without seeing him that it was Guy. Something warm fluttered in her belly, but she ignored it and rushed to the bars.

Her breath caught in her throat the moment he came into view.

Even in his plain, crisp uniform, he looked incredible. She'd almost forgotten how handsome he was, with his short brown hair and moss-green eyes. He hadn't changed much these past two years, but there was still something different about him…a sort of hardness in his face that she wasn't used to seeing. At least not directed at her.

Seconds turned into a full minute and they still hadn't spoken. Her tension soon turned into anxiety and she broke the silence between them. She wrapped her hands around the bars and tried to summon her confidence.

"Hello, Guy." She had hoped her tone would come out strong and assertive, but instead it came out tiny and unsure. She cleared her throat and tried again. "I'm so glad you're here." *Much better.*

Yet he remained silent and stone-still, not acknowledging any of her words. She sighed.

"I know this is a surprise, and that we have a lot to talk about. But first...can you please let me out of here?"

"Give me one good reason why I should." His tone was as harsh as his dark gaze.

"Because you know me. You know this has to be a big misunderstanding. Maybe I shouldn't have been speeding, and I certainly shouldn't have driven the car with those expired tags, but I don't deserve to be in here for that!"

He folded his arms across his chest. His stance said he was bracing for an argument. She should have known this wouldn't go over easy.

"Tell me, Mya. What is it you deserve, then? For me to carry you out of here? Tell you everything's going to be okay and that I'll take care of everything?" He suddenly came closer, the metal bars the only thing keeping them from touching. "Well, baby, that's just not going to happen."

She cringed inside at his unforgiving tone and harsh glare. Everything about him was...cold.

Is he that angry with me?

She remembered the warm smiles and tender looks whenever he would look at her. That was what she had come back for. That was what she wanted again.

"Guy, I know you're still mad. This is not how I wanted things to go today. This is certainly not how I wanted us to meet again." She motioned around the cell, her cuffs limiting her movements. "But we need to talk and I don't want to do it here."

His gaze lowered and his lips tightened. "Give me your hands."

Without hesitation, Mya slipped her cuffed hands through the small opening of the cell door. He gripped the metal restraints and began to undo the lock, careful not to touch her.

But she wanted his touch. She wanted to touch *him*. She didn't dare.

Staring at his bent head, she wondered what she could possibly say to make up for the pain she caused him.

"I'm sorry."

She hadn't meant to blurt out those exact words, but they felt right. She wasn't sorry for leaving—she had needed that moment away—but she was sorry for walking out on him like she had. If she could redo that night, maybe even talk to him first before disappearing, she would do it.

He slipped off the cuffs and tucked them behind his belt, never acknowledging her words.

"Guy? Did you hear me? I said I'm sorry."

He regarded her evenly. "I don't care."

Those cold words took the breath out of her. "You don't mean that."

"Then you don't know me."

"Yes, I do. I know you. I know you still care and that you're still pissed at me, and I'm sorry for that. If I could do it all again, I would!"

His gaze was like shards of ice. There was no forgiveness in them. "Which part? Walking out on me on our wedding night or never marrying me to begin with?"

She winced, shutting her eyes against the pain in his gruff voice. A pain he tried to mask.

"I was wrong for leaving like that. I should have handled things better, but that night I was so confused.

And after Dad…" She swallowed the lump in her throat. "I wanted to be with you, Guy. I did. But everything was moving too fast and I got scared. Couldn't you see that?"

"Don't you dare accuse me of pressuring you in this. We talked about getting married before."

"Yes, but—"

"And after the funeral, I asked what you wanted me to do to ease your pain. You said you wanted us to always be together. You asked me to keep my promise to you." His voice was low, measured. "I did."

Mya glanced away. "Yes, you did, and I don't regret that part. But when you promised we would get married, I never thought it would be at a courthouse thirty miles outside of town. That was not what I wanted."

His jaw clenched. "So because I couldn't give you a lavish wedding, you left me?"

A twinge of anger bristled inside her. "No, I left because I had just buried my dad and I needed time to mourn him!"

Heavy silence settled between them and she immediately regretted her outburst.

"You weren't the only one grieving him, Mya."

She stared at him searchingly, realizing how selfish she had been. In her misery, she had only thought about her grief. She knew the bond her father and Guy had shared, yet had been completely absorbed with her own pain.

"You're right," she whispered. "I should have been there for you."

"We should have been there for each other. That's what couples do."

"Okay, I'm here now. Let me be there for you. Let me fix *us*."

He shook his head, his expression guarded. "We don't need fixing. We just need to put an end to this phony marriage."

She sucked in a breath, stung by his rash words. Was that what he wanted? Tears clouded her vision and she quickly blinked them away.

"Guy, that's not what I want. I know I made some mistakes, but you were never one of them."

"Yet it took you two fucking years to decide you wanted to stay married to me."

Stony silence fell between them again. She clung to the bars, her grip unbearably tight around the cold rods. For a moment she was stunned. In all the years she'd known him, he'd never cursed at her.

He really had changed.

"I've always wanted to be married to you, Guy," she murmured. "I just wasn't ready then."

"And I'm supposed to be thrilled you finally made up your mind?"

No, you're supposed to tell me how much you love and missed me.

There was a tightening in her chest, but she ignored it. She wouldn't let him leave here thinking she wanted their marriage dissolved. "You remembered what you promised me that night you gave me this?"

Reaching into the front of her blouse, she pulled out the thin chain that held two entwined hearts at its center. His eyes fell to the necklace he had given her a long time ago—on their first Valentine's Day as a couple.

His expression remained stoic as he stared down at it. It had been the equivalent of his "promise ring" to her, and she wouldn't let him forget that.

"That night, you promised that nothing would ever come between us, that you would love and protect me always." She clutched the small jewel. "You made me your wife and I accepted you as my husband. I plan to hold you to that promise."

His eyes narrowed. "Why?"

"Because I love you. I'm still in love with you. I came back here for *you*."

The grim lines around his mouth tightened. She stared at him, silently pleading him to forgive her. Instead, he turned his face away for a moment. Suddenly, he shook his head, as if resolving some internal conflict.

"You don't love me, Mya. You don't just walk out on the person you love. I don't know why you came back here, but it wasn't for me."

Her shoulders fell. She'd been naive to think this would be easy. Leaving him had never been a simple decision, but he couldn't understand that. He hadn't felt trapped that night. It may not have been his intention, but that was how she had felt.

Trapped.

As trapped as she did now in this cell.

Suddenly, a rush of cold air blew from the old vents and brushed against her back. She shivered, wanting more than anything in that moment to be free of her prison. Her eyes fell to his collar, a small reprieve from his cold stare.

"Are you going to let me out of here?"

Guy hesitated for a moment then sifted through a ring of keys. She could feel his eyes on her as he unlocked the heavy door. As soon as it opened, she released a small sigh of relief. But her relief was short-lived when she realized there were no longer any barriers between them. He stepped back and held the cell door open for her.

She kept her gaze locked with his as she stepped out. She wanted very much to throw her arms around him, but he would most likely recoil from her touch, and she couldn't risk the humiliation. She took another step toward him. He didn't move.

His nostrils flared and she came closer. She recognized the dark intensity in his gaze. He had that same look in his eyes when she had stolen her first kiss from him. She had just turned eighteen and may have been inexperienced where men were concerned, but she knew then, as she knew now, that she wanted him.

And he still wanted her.

A heady warmth emanated from his large body. Despite the hard set of his mouth, there was a slight softening of his eyes as he continued to stare down at her. Compelled by a force beyond her control, Mya reached out to touch him.

"Guy, I…"

To her chagrin, he jerked away from her. "Let's go."

She started down the long corridor and he followed behind her, keeping distance between them. She felt the silence swelling up, demanding to be filled, but she couldn't find any words that didn't seem hollow.

How was she supposed to reach him when he kept this hard, invisible wall between them?

They passed a large chamber that held a man who sat slouched on the bench inside. His hooded eyes appeared bloodshot and his beard was overgrown. Was the man drunk? At second glance, Mya recognized who sat slouched inside and stopped.

"Is that Jackson?"

"Yeah," was all Guy offered. "Keep moving."

She ignored his command. Last she remembered, the two men had been good friends. Jackson may have been something of a troublemaker, but nothing that would get him put in here.

Unless he had done something worth being in a cell for.

"Why is he in there?"

"None of your business. Now keep moving."

Her back drew up at Guy's blunt response, but she continued down the hall. Apparently, he had no qualms about having her arrested, and his friends were no exception.

They made their way back into the station and she avoided looking at the other officers.

"Wait here."

Mya fell into the bench seat along the wall and watched as Guy made his way to Officer Justice. Her eyes were trained on his broad back and rigid shoulders as he spoke to the deputy. He was different. Not that he had ever been the carefree, laid-back type, but he had never been this...detached.

Guy had a quick discussion with the deputy, who turned to look at her. The man nodded then rose from his desk. They exchanged a few more words before Guy left, not sparing her another glance.

Mya's heart fell.

Was that it? Was he really just going to turn his back on her?

Like you did him.

Guilt once again assailed her. She couldn't blame him for not welcoming her back with open arms. She had messed things up between them and he was obviously still hurt, though he would never admit it. She would just have to find a way to make up for it and fix things between them.

"Ms. Daniels?"

Mya started, not realizing Officer Justice was standing only two feet from where she sat.

"I was able to reach the previous owners and get everything cleared with your vehicle. It's against county law to drive an unregistered vehicle with expired tags, but we're letting you off with a warning. The sheriff asked me to bring you by the municipal office, and then we'll pick up your vehicle."

Mya rose to her feet and glanced at the office Guy had disappeared into. "Can I speak to him?"

The deputy shifted uncomfortably. "He has a lot of work to get back to. Maybe try him again later…"

Mya noted the pity in his pale brown eyes and her cheeks warmed with embarrassment.

"Sure," she muttered. "If it's all right with you, then, I'd like to leave now."

Four

FROM HIS OFFICE WINDOW, Guy caught a glimpse of Mike leading Mya out of the station. She glanced back at their small building then froze. Through the distance, their eyes met and a bolt of desire shot through him.

She was still beautiful.

Her smooth skin gleamed in the late afternoon sun like polished rosewood. Her full lips were slightly parted and all he could think about was how soft and sweet they had once felt against his.

A stab of longing shot through him and he turned away from the window. He fell into his seat, willing the heavy beating of his heart to slow. Even in the solitude of his office, he couldn't quite relax.

The station was strangely quiet, but internally Guy was still reeling from seeing her again. The tense moment in the jail cell replayed in his head. Seeing her hadn't been enough. He wanted to touch her, taste her. Resisting the urge had been damn near impossible, but he had managed. Barely.

Guy cursed and leaned back into his seat. She brought up all the old feelings he'd taken two long years to bury. Yet today, he discovered just how weak he was where she was concerned and he hated the feeling. He needed to remember how easy it had been for her to discard her feelings for him, how easy it had been for her to leave him on a night that had been their first time as husband and wife.

Hell, it had been their first time, period.

Making love to her that long-ago night was still imprinted in his memory. She, on the other hand, had not felt any of the ecstasy he had coming into her for the first time. He could still remember the way her warmth wrapped tightly around him, the way her breath had brushed against his neck, the sweet sounds of her moans… Guy shifted in his seat, the thought of that night only adding to his discomfort.

Along with those powerful memories was the one he couldn't forget—the one when he'd discovered her gone, the mildly cool bed sheet still warm from her nude body.

Yet even with that reminder, Guy still craved her.

"Damn it," he muttered.

He couldn't weaken in his resolve. He may not know why she'd returned to Cedar Bend, but he was certain it had more to do with her selfish needs than it did because of her supposed love for him.

Whatever her reason, Guy wouldn't be duped again. It had taken him a broken heart to realize they weren't compatible with each other. She didn't want him the way he wanted her, and he would be damned if he was trapped in an unhappy marriage.

Now that she was back, he needed to make time to file for that annulment. His heart twisted at the thought, but it needed to be done. He'd given himself enough excuses these past two years. If he really wanted to move on with his life—move on from *her*—he needed to put an end to this charade.

There was also his mother and the risk of her finding out. She would be heartbroken—and pissed—that they had gotten married without involving her. And he didn't want to hurt his mother. It was a wonder she hadn't already found out with the constant communication she'd had with Mya.

Guy straightened in his seat, a small jolt passing through him as he came to a sudden realization. If anyone had known about Mya's surprise return, it would be his sweet, impulsive, meddlesome mother.

The two of them spoke—a lot—and yet his mother failed to mention this bit of news to him. Guy didn't bother masking his irritation when he reached for the phone and dialed his mother's cell. Maybe now he could find out what Mya was really doing back at Cedar Bend.

His mother answered on the second ring, and he said without preamble, "Ma, you should have told me."

"Guy Gregory Lawson, have you gotten so disrespectful you forgot how to greet your mother?"

He blew out an exasperated breath. "Hi, Ma."

"Much better. Now tell me what you're going on about?"

"Mya. She's in town. Why didn't you tell me she was coming back?"

"Well, why should I have? You made it very plain last time I brought her up that you didn't want me talking about her."

"No, I said I wanted you to stop riding me for not answering her calls." He may have been purposely avoiding Mya's calls, but it irritated the hell out of him that his mother would accuse him of being unreasonable. "She had her chance to say whatever she needed to say *before* she left the country."

And before she left my bed.

His mother made a sound of disapproval. "I wish you would let that go. It's not attractive when a guy your age holds a grudge."

Guy gritted his teeth. This was why he avoided talking about Mya when it came to his mother. The two of them had a special bond—much like he had with Mya's father—and his mother would naturally assume he was just holding a silly grudge, when it went so much deeper than that.

"Could you at least tell me what she's doing back here?"

"If you know she's in town, I assume you spoke with her, so why didn't you ask her yourself?"

"I did."

"And…"

Guy hesitated. "I didn't get a straight enough answer."

"Well, then if you must know, she's going to be helping me run the shop. She knows the situation and has offered to help me part-time until I can hire someone full-time again."

Guy frowned. So that's what it was. For a moment, Guy had wondered if Mya told his mother the same thing she had confessed in the jail cell.

I love you. I'm still in love with you. I came back here for you.

Maybe telling him what she thought he wanted to hear had been her angle in getting out of that cell.

But isn't that what you want to hear?

Guy shook his head, annoyed by the fleeting thought. If there were any truth to those words, he refused to acknowledge it.

"Ma, did you tell her you couldn't afford to pay her?"

"She knows. We've made an arrangement, so don't you worry. Neither one of us are going to be a burden to you. I'm just excited to have help again, and also have our girl back. So tell me. How is she?"

"Fine."

His mother blew out a loud, exasperated breath. "You haven't seen her in two years and that's all you can say. I want to know how she looks. Does she seem happy to be back?"

"You'll have to see her for yourself then, Ma. I have to get back to work."

Guy hung up the phone, but getting back to his duties proved to be impossible as his mind wandered to thoughts of her again.

How did she look?

As stunning as he remembered.

Was she happy to be back?

He had no clue…

If he had to guess, then the answer would be a resounding no. And he would have only himself to blame. Behind those big brown eyes of hers was a sadness that he'd seen before. But this time, he was responsible for putting that look in her eyes.

Guilt spread through him as he recalled every harsh, angry word he'd spoken to her. Though he stood by much of what he'd said, he resented the way in which he'd delivered them.

This was why they couldn't be together.

Not only did she still wield enough power to hurt him, she also had the ability to bring out the worst in him.

Mya walked into the small auto shop and was assaulted by a faint odor of motor oil and rubber. Behind the counter was a familiar, handsome face that broke into a wide grin.

"So it's true. You really are back."

Mya smiled. "That was fast. How did you find out?"

Damian Carson smirked. "Word gets around fast here."

He came from around the counter and pulled her into a hug. "Welcome home, Mya."

Though she yearned to hear those same words from Guy, it was nice to see that someone other than Gloria was happy to see her again.

Despite the dirt and grime on his dark blue coveralls, she returned his friendly embrace. This was the homecoming she had been hoping for.

"Thanks, Damian." She pulled away from him and glanced around the shop. She hadn't come into his family auto shop often, but it was apparent that organization wasn't his priority. "Where's Pops?"

"He's home. Resting. It's just me running the shop today."

"Oh, okay... Now it all makes sense."

He cocked his brow. "What does?"

She waved her hand around the store. "Why does the place look like it's been hit by a hurricane?"

The corner of his mouth quirked up and he sauntered back behind the counter. "Hey, if you're looking for work, I could always use the help."

"Sorry. I already have a job."

"Already? Didn't you just get back today?"

"I did, but I'm going to be working at the boutique again with Gloria. And doing other things. But if you really need the help, you should put up a Help Wanted sign."

Damian nodded dismissively. "Does Guy know you're back?"

Mya tensed at the mention of him. The car ride with Officer Justice—or Mike, as he insisted she call him—had been uncomfortable enough as it was. Not only did she have the misfortune of meeting Guy's second cousin under awkward circumstances, she also had an unsettling feeling that he knew more about her and Guy's situation than he let on. If she hadn't feared she would say too much, she would have asked him outright.

Besides, there was no way he knew. Everyone in town may have expected they would get married someday, but no one had a clue they had already made the commitment. Not even Gloria. It had been the hardest thing Mya had been forced to keep from her. Guy had mentioned annulling their marriage. She wondered if that was why he hadn't told his mother. The thought sent a wave of overwhelming sadness through her.

"I'm guessing from that look on your face that he doesn't?"

Mya blinked, pulling herself out of her bleak thoughts. "No, he knows."

"Have you talked to him?"

"I've tried."

Damian studied her for a moment. At first she thought he would change the subject, but she should have known better. Damian and Guy had gone to school together and been good friends. Naturally, he would be curious about what led to her leaving.

"Keep trying. He probably won't tell you this, but he missed the hell out of you while you were gone."

A glimmer of hope sprang in her. "Did he say that?"

Amusement flashed in his dark face. "If I could ever get him drunk, I'm sure he would have. But we all can see it. He can be a hard-ass sometimes, but don't give up on him."

She grinned. "I won't."

For the first time since she'd left the station, she started to feel better about her prospects in getting her Guy back.

"Good. Now let's go get you that car."

Damian led her outside, behind the auto shop. Parked beside his large pick-up truck with the faded words *Carson's Auto Shop* printed on the side sat her newly purchased, yet very old Jeep Wrangler.

"When you get a chance, you should bring it back in and let me look at it," he advised, handing her the keys.

"That clanging under the hood doesn't sound very good."

She sighed. *Great.* "I just bought this today. I was hoping I could get a few months out of it before I needed to get it serviced."

"I wouldn't wait that long, if I were you. Cars should purr, not squawk. And if it sounds like a duck…"

"It's probably my Jeep," she finished dryly.

He chuckled then turned back to study her car. "Some old things just aren't made to last forever."

Her hand unconsciously came up to her necklace as she studied the car as well.

But some old things are.

Five

THE SUN WAS BARELY PEEKING from the sky when Mya finally pulled up to her father's home. She was stunned by the sight before her. She expected the lawn to be overgrown and unattended, but she didn't expect the house to look so…abandoned.

The old two-story home looked like something out of a horror movie. Evening was approaching and the large overgrown trees cast eerie shadows around it. There was no sign of life, and worse, it looked condemned.

Mya climbed out of the Jeep and took cautious steps toward the place, careful to watch her steps.

What happened?

Nothing, that's what.

And it was her fault. In her haste to get away from the one place she had called home for fifteen years, she had not only abandoned Guy but also left behind her father and his memory. This had been their home since her mother had left Cedar Bend and moved back to England, giving her father complete custody. At six years old, Mya hadn't quite understood what her mother's abandonment had meant.

Eventually, she had grown accustomed to not seeing her mother every day. Her father had made a life for them in this old house, and they had been happy. Mya had never wanted for anything, and her father made her feel loved and protected.

Just as Guy did.

In turn, she had let her father's home turn into this— a gloomy, broken shell of its former self…

Mya pushed the depressing thought aside and walked up the porch, the boards beneath her feet creaking loudly. Inside the house was in better condition, but not by much. There was a stale odor that hung in the air, and every step she took, the wood floors groaned.

She mechanically flipped on the lights, but there was nothing.

Of course.

She didn't know why she expected electricity. The house was uninhabitable, with absolutely no signs of life. Looking around her old home, Mya realized just how poor a job she had done in preserving her father's legacy and his memory.

Was that how Guy felt? That she had turned her back on their love, that she had forgotten and abandon him? Mya sighed. Maybe she had abandoned him, but she had never forgotten him.

She could never do that.

Making her way through each room on the first floor, Mya noted the peeling and cracked paint. She stopped at the foot of the stairs. Did she dare go up? The century-old home had always shown signs of its age before, and she couldn't be sure what repairs were needed now.

She needed to do something, though.

This house had been in her father's family since its construction, and it would have eventually become hers to pass down to her children. Yet she hadn't given the place a second thought when she'd left for England.

An overwhelming sense of guilt and loneliness came over her, and Mya rushed out of the ramshackle place. She couldn't stay here. What was once a home wasn't anymore. She wasn't sure if it would ever be again.

Mya climbed back into her car and sat there, uncertain of her next move. She could go to Guy, but after today, space was what they needed. Once he got used to her being back, she would get in touch with him again.

Then there was Gloria. She had no doubt that the older woman would welcome her in, but Mya didn't want to be in the awkward position of explaining how she had let her father's home collapse into such a deplorable condition—or have her ask why she hadn't gone to Guy first.

Gloria had asked her once before what happened between them and Mya had given her default answer.

It was complicated.

That left their town's only bed and breakfast, which was the closest thing to a motel in Cedar Bend. And staying there would raise even more questions Mya wasn't prepared to answer.

Recognizing her limited choices, she called Gloria.

"Mya, honey, I was wondering when you were going to call me. I spoke with Guy earlier and he told me you'd arrived today."

"He did?" Mya wondered if he'd also mentioned her brief stint at the jail. "What else did he say?"

"Not much else. He's excited to see you back."

"He said that?"

"In so many words."

Mya frowned. The way Guy had turned his back on her at the station proved exactly how he felt about her. Unfortunately, Gloria wanted to hear what she wanted to hear.

"So how are you settling in?"

Mya sighed and explained in limited detail the situation she found herself in. "Needless to say, I can't stay here. Not until I can get someone to check out what kind of repairs are needed."

"I'm sorry, honey. I didn't realize it was in such bad condition. We had that terrible tropical storm last summer. I'm sure that only made things worse."

Mya glimpsed up at the house. The large crack running just below the roof stared back at her like an ominous smirk.

"Gloria, I really hate to ask, but could I stay with you for few days? Just until I can find another place to crash?"

There was a short pause before Gloria spoke again. "I'm sorry, honey, but I've had Guy's old room renovated into a mini gym. Well, it started off that way. Now it's my storage room. You wouldn't be comfortable here. But Guy has plenty of space. Have you asked him?"

Mya's hand tightened around her cell. "No, I don't think—"

"Call him, dear. I'm sure he wouldn't have any problem taking you in. Now I have to run. It's crochet night tonight. I'll see you tomorrow. Love you!"

Gloria hung up before Mya could get out another word. She stared at her phone, stunned. If she wasn't mistaken, she would have sworn Gloria had purposely rushed her off the phone.

With one last glance at the house, Mya released a small sigh of resignation and started her car. She didn't know how Guy would react. He could very well tell her to leave.

That was a chance she would just have to take.

Besides, she had to face him again sometime soon.

Why not tonight?

Guy pulled up next to the Jeep Wrangler in his driveway and muttered a curse. On his patio, sat Mya perched on a mountain of luggage. It wasn't a hard guess as to why she was here. He'd driven past her father's home enough to know the condition it had fallen into. But there had been nothing he could do about it. Now she needed a place to stay.

But why him? Did she just enjoy driving him crazy?

Guy got out of his truck and stopped in front of the low steps. There was no way he could have her near, much less under the same roof with him.

"Mya, you can't stay here."

"Why not?"

Guy gritted his teeth. "You know why."

She pushed away from her bags and came to stand at the top of the steps, directly in front of him. "How are we supposed to work on our marriage if you keep pushing me away?"

"There's nothing to work on. I told you that. We should have annulled this sham of a marriage years ago."

The moment you left for England.

"If that's what you wanted, why didn't you?"

His mouth snapped shut. The unexpected question took him off guard, but it wasn't something he hadn't thought before. He'd given himself a mountain of excuses before, but it all boiled down to the fact that he had always held out hope. He'd wanted to believe that she would realize her mistake and come back to him. He'd had countless fantasies about her just like this. Waiting for him… Coming back to him…

But a long time had passed since that delusion, and eventually the fantasies had faded. He'd stopped pining for that moment, accepting the cold reality that she had left him and was never coming back.

Mya came down one step and stood only inches away from him. She took hold of his hand, and he stiffened as her soft palm brought back memories he wanted to forget.

"I think you didn't do it because you still love me and you want us to work."

Guy stared into her warm maple-brown eyes as indecision warred inside him. He did still love her, damn it. But he also knew they were too different to ever be able to work. He needed someone who was certain of herself—someone who wouldn't run away when things got a little tough.

He pulled his hand out of hers. "You should call my mother. You'll be more comfortable there."

Moving around her, he bounded up the short steps. She followed closely behind him.

"I did call her. She doesn't have room for me."

He ignored her, quickly working the front door lock.

"*Guy.*"

At her forceful tone, he stopped short. His hand stilled on the doorknob, but he didn't turn around.

"Please. I have nowhere else to go."

His lips tightened. Of course she didn't. Because of her neglect, her father's house was in shambles. The few times he'd driven past it had been a harsh reminder of how little thought she must have given any of them.

Yet, as usual, she was looking for him to rescue her. But if she thought he would go on pretending as if they were in a real marriage, she would be sadly mistaken.

Guy pushed the door open then went to grab her bags.

"You can take the guest room in the back. For tonight."

Mya rolled into a tighter ball on the full-size bed, trying to ward off the chill in the cold, drafty room. Sleep eluded her—not because she couldn't seem to get warm enough, but because the man she loved was only a few feet away from her.

Yet he might as well be an ocean away.

She hadn't expected him to put her in the guest room, but then again, she shouldn't be surprised. The only thing that gave her hope was knowing he still did love her.

He hadn't denied it when she'd brought it up to him, and from the way he hesitated when she confronted him, she knew he was stubbornly fighting his attraction to her.

He had ignored her most of the evening, spending most of his time in his bedroom, while she had tried making herself comfortable in this cold room.

But there was no getting comfortable. She was freezing and miserable, and no adjusting of the thermostat would push the heat to the back room where she slept.

After an hour of the discomfort, Mya got out of bed and went searching for something heavier than the thin sheet that was doing a poor job keeping the chill out. But this wasn't her home, and she realized she didn't know where something as simple as blankets were.

"This is ridiculous," she muttered.

She didn't understand why she had to act like a stranger in her husband's home. The need for warmth propelled her to action, and before Mya could reconsider her next move, she found herself padding down the hall to Guy's bedroom.

The bedroom they had spent their first night as husband and wife.

Mya slowly turned the knob and waited until her eyes adjusted to the dimness before she made her way to the bed.

Guy slept on his stomach, his tousled head turned toward her. She stood there for a moment, taking in the beautiful sight before her. She liked him this way. His guard was down and he appeared less formidable without the scowl that seemed to attach itself to his brow whenever he looked at her.

Mya pulled back the covers and climbed into bed beside him. His heat was magnetic, and she cuddled closer.

She didn't have time to savor the moment, however, before he jerked awake.

"What the— Mya?"

"Yes?" She forced nonchalance in her voice, even though her heart was racing. Would he demand that she get the hell out of his bed? The same bed she'd lost her virginity.

"What happened? What's wrong?"

At the obvious concern in his voice, she couldn't help but smile. "I think the heater's broken in the guest room. I got cold."

He didn't say anything for a heartbeat, as if he was processing her words, then he reached over and turned on the bedside lamp.

A soft glow illuminated the room and she could see him clearly. His jaw was covered with a day-old beard. With a low groan, he fell on his back and rubbed a hand over his face.

"I'll look into it this weekend. Do you want me to grab the space heater?"

Mya propped herself up and leaned over him. "You don't have to. This bed is big enough for the both of us."

He removed his hand from his eyes and stared up at her, his moss-green eyes guarded. "That's not a good idea."

"Why?"

His jaw tightened. "You know why."

"Is it because you won't be able to keep your hands off me?"

The muscles in his jaw flexed again, but she didn't need his words to know she was right. His silent response was answer enough.

She placed her hand on his bare chest and leaned down lower. "What if I don't want you to?"

He covered her hand with his and tightened his grip. "Mya——"

Moving with an impulse that surprised her, she kissed him—kissed him in the way she had anticipated since she'd driven into town. Slow and lingering… Her lips moved over his until he relaxed under the pressure. She kept her lips fitted against his, remembering their shape and savoring his taste.

He brought his hands up behind her neck, and for a moment, she thought he would push her away. But to her surprise, he flipped her onto her back and moved over her, deepening the kiss. She wrapped her arms and legs around him, welcoming his hard warmth pressing her into the soft mattress.

Memories of their first time together flooded her, and a different kind of heat began to wash through her. He'd been so gentle with her, yet the passion between them had still burned bright.

What she would give to have that moment again.

Cupping her breast, he molded his palm around it, gently squeezing her as he kissed down the length of her neck. A soft sigh of pleasure escaped her.

He sucked gently at the sensitive flesh at her throat before moving down the soft curve of her shoulder. Desire licked its way up Mya's heated body, and her sighs soon became fervent moans.

Suddenly, Guy froze above her and pulled back the thin strap of her camisole. "What's this?"

She was so immersed in the tidal wave of pleasure that it took her a moment to register his question. Mya blinked up at him, but his gaze was transfixed on the tattoo on her shoulder blade.

"They're feathers."

"I can see that. But…why?"

She shrugged. She could understand his surprise. Small town girls didn't go out getting inked, especially not on such a visible area of the body.

"I got it because I liked it. It reminds me that I'm not a caged bird anymore."

He went rigid above her, and she was surprised by the sudden change in him.

"Was the idea of marriage to me so bad?"

His gruff words struck her to her core.

"Oh, Guy. It wasn't ever about you," she began, placing her hand lightly on his cheek. "I just—"

He pulled away from her touch and rolled out of bed. "You can sleep in here. I'll take the other room."

Mya watched as he left the bedroom, her heart sinking. She curled onto her side, trying to suppress the frustration and misery that threatened to consume her.

Six

"MA, she can't stay with me." Guy pinched the bridge of his nose, trying to ease the pressure that was starting to settle there.

"Then where do you want her to stay?"

"I don't know. She should have thought of that before she showed up."

"She didn't just 'show up.' Mya's been planning to come back for three months now. You would know that if you had bothered to talk to her while she'd been away."

Guy ignored his mother's pointed comment. "And in all that planning, she couldn't bother to secure a place to stay? Or had she really expected me to just welcome her back with open arms?"

"That would be nice. Remember how very close you two were, *before* you started dating? I don't understand why you're being so hard on her."

"I'm not. I'm simply saying that she can't live with me."

His mother sighed. "So you'd let her stay in that old house, which is practically falling apart? Or should she go live with her old friends… Then again, that would only fuel the gossip about you too.

Guy frowned. *What gossip?*

"I suppose she could stay at the shop, but the accommodations would be quite uncomfortable. And unpleasant."

"I know what you're doing, Ma. But I'm serious. She can't stay with me."

"Can't you do this for me, then? Your only mother. I'm not asking you to marry her. Just give her a place to lay her head."

Guy tensed at those choice words. His mother may not be asking them to get married, but she was asking for something far more impossible. Last night was a testament to that.

How was he supposed to keep Mya at arm's length if just the sight of her made him want to give in to her spell? He needed to figure out the endgame to their situation, and fast.

Last night, he'd almost lost his control, with the feel of her soft lips and warm body pressed beneath him. Even now, his shaft lengthened just thinking about her touch. If he let her stay, he was only inviting trouble—not only to his piece of mind, but also his heart.

"Ma, I can't. Things between me and Mya aren't the same. It's best if we just keep our distance."

"What happened between you two? You don't tell me anything anymore, and ever since Mya left—to be with her mother, I might add—it's like you have this big chip on your shoulder."

Guy's grip tightened around the phone. He wondered, if he told his mother the truth right now, would she think he was still being unreasonable?

Who was he kidding?

He wouldn't tell her anything. She would be pissed—and hurt—that not only was she not involved, but that he had kept it from her these past two years. Besides, he couldn't see his farce of a marriage continuing much longer, so there was no need to upset her.

"You can stop wondering about us, Ma. It's old history. Now if you—"

"Old, ha! You've been pining for Mya for the past two years, and now that you have a chance to be together again, you're practically pushing her away."

Silence fell between them. Had he been so obvious? Guy had tried to bury himself in his work, hoping to forget her, hoping to put his wasted energy longing for her into better use. Like serving and protecting his town.

His mother's weary sigh was distinct over the phone. "How did I ever raise you to be so stubborn?"

"You wouldn't understand, Ma. You never had someone walk out on you like she did me."

There was another deep silence before his mother spoke again. "How dare you say that? Do you forget how your bastard father abandoned us?"

"That's different."

"Why? Because we weren't married? That didn't mean I loved the bastard any less."

"I mean that—" Guy caught himself before he could let the words slip out.

I mean you were never deserted on your wedding night.

His mother's voice softened. "Guy, please reconsider. Mya's a good girl and she needs you. Besides, she's here to help me. You should be falling over your feet, begging her to stay."

"I think I'll skip that part," he said dryly.

"And now that she's back, you'll have someone to take to Eric's wedding," Gloria continued, ignoring him. Then she added tersely, "I can't believe you let Eric Benson get married before you."

Guy bit back a retort. The thought of his friend's upcoming wedding reminded him of Eric's party this weekend—and Mayor Powers' unexpected invite to his function next Friday. As reluctant as Guy was to attend, he knew he would have to make an appearance at the mayor's dinner party.

Maybe having Mya near would turn out to be useful after all. Guy was tired of the mayor shoving his daughter in his direction and putting him in the awkward position of turning the young woman down. With Mya at his side, the mayor could finally stop trying to start something that wasn't there.

"Fine. I'll let her stay."

"That's my boy," his mother practically gushed. "I knew you would do the right thing. And you'll see. This will be good for you both."

"Don't get too excited, Ma. This is only temporary."

"Yes, yes. But while you're together, maybe you can finally work out whatever issues you two are having so I can finally get some damn grandbabies."

The line was abruptly disconnected and Guy could only stare blankly at the phone.

Mya walked down the path toward her father's plot, vaguely remembering it from the album of pictures that had been shoved in front of her during the worst time of her life. She reached the low headstone and was disheartened to see the dirt and bare branches that had gathered around.

"Oh, Daddy."

With a low sob, she fell to her knees and began brushing away at the dirt and fallen leaves. Mya placed the small bouquet of flowers she had brought with her over his plot and sat back on her haunches.

Her heart ached still for her father, but she needed to be here. The last time she had been at her father's gravesite was during the funeral. She had been surrounded by faces she couldn't remember. The only person she had been aware of was Guy. He had been by her side the entire time, his warmth and strength a comfort she desperately needed. He'd been there from the moment they had called her to the hospital—and the night they pronounced her father dead.

Her world had changed forever that night.

At twenty-one, Mya hadn't been prepared to lose another parent. When her mother decided to remarry and move back to England, she had been too young to understand that her mother wouldn't be in her life like mothers should be. But with Gloria's help, her father had done the best he could raising a daughter on his own.

With her father, Mya had never felt unwanted or unloved, but losing him had stripped away the protective layers that kept her shielded for so long. She had been an unapologetic, spoiled daddy's girl, and losing the first man she'd ever loved was unbearable.

But in the two years she'd spent away, the pain of his lost was no longer the crushing blow it once was. She still hurt, but she had all the happy memories to comfort her—and the practical memories to remind her of just how much he cared.

Her father's deep voice and carefully chosen words about her relationship with Guy replayed in her head, and Mya found herself lost in the memory of their last dinner together…

"Sweetie, I know how much you and Guy love each other, but I'm just suggesting that you don't rush into anything. You're almost twenty-one. You should leave Cedar Bend and go see the rest of the world. Maybe even go to college. Then when you get back, you can get married and settle down with Guy and your five kids."

There was a twinkle in her dad's dark eyes, and Mya couldn't help but return his smile. "We love each other, Daddy, but no one's rushing into marriage anytime soon."

"Are you sure? I see the way he looks at you. He's eager to get you out of my house so he can have you all to himself."

"Daddy!"

Mya's cheeks burned, but there was some truth to her dad's words. Guy had been dropping a lot of hints about them getting married, and she wondered when he would make his move and ask her already.

"You're an adult now, Mya, and I can see how much Guy cares about you. I know some day you'll be moving on with a family of your own, but you have the rest of your life to raise one. It doesn't have to be now."

Mya stared at her father across the table, a bit concerned by how adamant his words were. "Why do I have the feeling you don't want us together?"

"It's not that, sweetie. I just don't want you to feel pressured into anything. I can see that you two love each other, but you're also in different places in life. A man like Guy may not be able to give you the things you want if you don't really know what that is."

"I do know what I want, Daddy." Mya bit her lip, realizing how false those words appeared. She was indeed about to turn twenty-one and was still working at Gloria's boutique with no clear plans to do much else. "It may not look like it, but I do. And I know I want to be here with you, with Guy."

Her father nodded, but his eyes bored into hers. Mya shifted uncomfortably in her seat.

"Where is all this coming from anyway? I thought you liked Guy."

"I do, honey. Guy is one of the good ones, which is why I don't want you two to go through what I went through with your mother."

Mya frowned, offended by the comparison. "Daddy, I would never leave Guy like that. I have no reason to. I love him and he makes me happy."

Her dad shrugged. "I thought the same thing about your mother, but she wasn't cut out for small town life, and for six years, she'd been miserable. I don't want that for you and Guy."

Mya smiled reassuringly at him and reached across the table to take his hand. "Well, you're worrying for nothing. This is my home. All I know is Cedar Bend. I have no plans to leave here."

Yet she had.

She'd done exactly to Guy what her mother had done to her father. It wasn't a conscientious decision, but she had left him. At the time, she only wanted to be alone, to sort through her thoughts and emotions. Yet when her mother called with an invitation—and plane ticket—to come to England, Mya hadn't hesitated.

She had left without a second thought.

What should have been a short trip had turned into months and then years, only because her mother had talked her into staying longer. And with their tenuous relationship budding, Mya hadn't wanted to disappoint her.

But if she'd had her way, Mya would have come back to Cedar Bend much sooner. And maybe she and Guy would have started on those five kids her father liked to tease her about.

The corners of her lips lifted slightly and she rested her hand on the headstone, suddenly feeling at peace—and closer to her father than she had in a long time. Without meaning to, she had heeded his advice and gone to see more of the world. She only wished she had done so before she and Guy had exchanged generic vows.

"You were right, Daddy. I shouldn't have rushed into things. I needed to get away. And I did. I've been to England and have seen places that I've only read about. But I'm home now and I'm here to stay."

Mya closed her eyes and turned her face up to the clear blue sky, inhaling deeply.

This was her home. Her heart was here. She belonged *here*.

Seven

"MYA, would you hurry up? We're going to be late."

She came out of the bedroom, putting on the backs to her earrings. Guy stopped his pacing and gaped at her. His gaze moved down her body.

Guy tried to mask his reaction but failed. Just when he thought she couldn't get any more beautiful, she came out wearing a dress like that—a deep violet dress that hugged her curves. It was a far cry from the flowy skirts and simple tops she typically wore.

In that dress, he could make out every dip of her curves, from her medium-sized breasts that fit neatly in his palms to the round flare of her hips. Guy wasn't sure what he wanted most—to take her out and show her off, or carry her into his bedroom and strip off every figure-hugging layer.

"We don't actually need to be there on time, Guy. It's a party, not an appointment." She came to where he stood in front of the door and froze. "What?"

Guy shook his head. Showing her off would have to do. Besides, it was the main reason why he'd invited her to come to the party with him. The good people of Cedar Bend loved good gossip, and once everyone saw

Mya on his arms, maybe the mayor would set his unscrupulous sights on another sap to marry his daughter off to.

"Do I look okay?"

You look beautiful.

From her flawlessly made-up face to the curls piled stylishly atop her head, he could see what the influences of her time outside their small town had done to her usual style.

He cleared his throat and made a show of glancing at his watch. "You look fine. Are you ready?"

The drive to the Benson mansion was a quiet one. He was acutely aware of Mya sitting beside him in his truck. He had the car radio playing the oldies just to fill in the silence.

Guy glanced over at her. She stared out the window, her hands folded on her lap, and seemed deep in thought. At that moment, he would have given anything to know what she was thinking. In the past, she had been a bubble of energy, filled with interesting, silly, or strange topics to talk about. He'd always been amazed at how she could go from talking world events one minute to chatting about what celebrity won which award at whatever award show.

Now she sat quietly beside him, more reserved than he'd known her to be. He wasn't sure if this new Mya was a result of her maturing or of her having spent the last two years in Europe, but there was a part of him that was nostalgic for the girl he'd once known.

The one he'd fallen in love with.

"Is Eric really running for mayor?"

Guy was surprised by the sudden question, then realized they were coming up to yet another "Vote for Eric Benson" sign.

"Yeah, he is. He announced it last year."

"So is this party tonight politically motivated?"

"It could be. It's an election year, so there's going to be a lot more of these social events from both sides."

"Wow. I never imagined he'd want to come back to Cedar Bend and become mayor, of all things."

"None of us did. Usually people who leave Cedar Bend…"

"Stay gone?" she finished.

"Yeah, they do," he said dryly.

"Well, I guess Eric and I are the exceptions."

"The only difference is that Eric went away to school. You just ran away."

He felt her eyes on him, but he kept his gaze fixed on the road ahead.

"And now I'm here to stay, Guy."

Silence once again fell between them. He didn't particularly care how she justified her leaving. The end result was that she had made the selfish decision to split, and that was that.

When they finally made it to the Benson mansion—a sprawling three-story house that could comfortably hold over seventy people and still give them room to spread out—the party was in full swing. They made it through the double doors and past the crush of people. A sudden protectiveness came over him, and Guy didn't want to let Mya out of his sight. He caught the looks they were getting from everyone, but it was the ogling from the men that bothered him the most.

Guy placed his hand on the small of her back and pulled her close. The possessive action was blatant, but he didn't care. He wanted it to be clear to every guy in the room that she belonged to him.

"Guy?"

He turned to the familiar voice and was surprised by the stunning woman behind him.

"Lori?"

Eric's twin sister pulled him into a tight hug. Guy was taken off guard for a moment but returned it affectionately.

"How've you been?"

She pulled back, but still held on to him. "I've been well. You?"

He shrugged. "Can't complain."

Lori Benson was the last person Guy had expected to see tonight, seeing as she was one of the few people who had left their small town and seemed content to stay away. In high school, they had dated casually, but parted friends when life took them on separate paths.

But Eric was her twin, so it wasn't a great surprise that she would come back to support her brother with his campaign run.

"It's really good to see you again, Guy."

"Hello, Lori."

Mya's terse greeting was unmistakable. Lori turned to her, a curious expression on her elegantly made-up face.

Instinctively, Guy pulled her to his side. "You remember Mya, don't you?"

Lori's sky-blue eyes widened with recognition. "Little Mya Daniels?" She sized her up, and Guy could sense Mya's growing tension. "I can't believe how much you've grown."

"So have you."

Guy blinked in surprise at Mya's flip words.

Lori plastered a smile on her lips, but her eyes were glacial. "Well, you're not a little girl anymore." She turned back to him and winked. "And you've managed to snag Cedar Bend's most eligible bachelor."

Mya took his hand and laced her fingers through his. "He hasn't been eligible for a while."

Lori glanced down at their locked hands, a challenging glint flashing in her eyes. "So I've heard... Does that mean you two will be following in Eric's footsteps down the aisle?"

"Actually, we're—"

He squeezed Mya's hand. "No one can follow in Eric's steps," he cut in briskly. "Where's the man of the hour, anyway?"

Guy could feel Mya's eyes on him but didn't turn to her. No way was he going to let her reveal their relationship in this crowded room just to piss Lori off.

"He's around somewhere. But first, let me introduce you to his fiancée. She's such a peach." Lori looped her arm around his and began tugging him away. "Do you mind if I steal him for a minute, Mya?"

Mya's hand fell away from his, and Guy was surprised at how much he missed her touch.

"He's all yours."

At those flat words, Guy realized then that he missed more than just her touch.

"Your misery is showing."

Startled, Mya turned to find Damian standing behind her. She was grateful to see a friendly face that wasn't secretly assessing her—or acting as if she were some strange object they didn't know how to handle.

"Is it that bad?"

He nodded, and her shoulders slumped. She wanted to feign cheerfulness, but it was hard to do when it was obvious her own husband was ignoring her. Not that anyone here knew they were married, and Guy had made it clear he wanted to keep it that way.

The way Lori practically threw herself on Guy, while undermining her, had left Mya furious and miserable at the same time. Now the pretentious woman had taken Guy somewhere, and she hadn't seen them since.

Misery tightened around Mya's chest. When Guy had invited her out tonight, she had held high hopes that things would be different, that he would open up again and make their relationship work.

So much for that.

"C'mon. Let's dance. Maybe I can shuffle a smile out of you tonight."

Mya let Damian guide her to the dance floor, ignoring the curious glances thrown their way. A slow dance number began playing, and he pulled her into a proper ballroom dance position. With his right hand on her upper back and their left hands clasped, Mya followed his lead around the room.

"I see someone has taken Mrs. Figaro's ballroom dancing class."

Damian laughed. "Yeah, I figured it couldn't hurt. Besides, Eric asked me to be in his wedding, so I get to finally put these skills to use."

"Well, I for one am grateful. I was really starting to feel like a leper in here."

"Don't," he said. "Everyone's just getting used to seeing you and Guy together again."

Mya frowned. "Why should it matter?"

"You know how folks in this town get. Whether you knew it or not, you and Guy were Cedar Bend's dream couple, and when you just left, well…"

Mya glanced up at him. "Well, what?"

He hesitated for a moment then said, "Some folks were kind of pissed with you. For a while, stories were going around that you left Guy for another guy." He chuckled at his pun. "Others just thought you went away to grieve, but when you never came back, they started to get other ideas."

Mya glanced around the room, suddenly feeling utterly exposed. She had grown up with these people, and they had turned on her, gossiping about her in the wake of her father's death. She shouldn't care what any of them thought, but she did.

Feeling the sting of a hundred judgmental eyes on her, Mya froze in the middle of the dance floor.

"Mya?"

She stepped out of his arms. "I'm sorry, Damian. I think I need some fresh air."

He followed her out the back of the house and to the large terrace. It wasn't until she was surrounded by the cool night air that she felt as if she could breathe again.

"Are you all right? Do you need me to get you anything?"

She shook her head. "No, thank you. I'm fine now."

Damian stuffed his hands in his pockets. "You know, you shouldn't let them get to you. No one here knows what you've been through. And it can't be easy losing your dad the way you did. If you needed to stay away for another ten years, I wouldn't blame you."

A lump formed in her throat and she blinked the tears away. There had never been an officer killed in the line of duty at Cedar Bend. That kind of stuff just didn't happen here. Having her father stabbed during a burglary gone wrong, and left to bleed to death, shouldn't have been his legacy. He should have grown old and retired like many of the town's sheriffs before him.

"Thanks, Damian. But I'm definitely here to stay."

The corner of his lips kicked up. "You, Mya Daniels, are much stronger than me."

Mya stared at him and recognized the sorrow that was hidden behind those coffee-dark eyes. She took his hand and gave it a reassuring squeeze.

"Is everything okay with Pops?"

For a moment, she saw the stark grief on his face, a grief she'd recognized in herself when her father had passed. It was no secret that his father was in poor health. Was Damian already grieving him?

He eventually returned her gentle squeeze with a solemn smile. "It's nothing we can't handle." Suddenly, a loud beeping disrupted the still air, and he glanced down at his watch. "I have to go now. Will you be okay?"

"Yes, I think I can go back and face them again."

"Good girl. And remember, you don't owe anyone in there a damn thing."

Her lips trembled slightly, but she was still able to manage a smile. "You're right." On impulse, she threw her arms around him and gave him a tight hug. "Thanks for keeping me company." Without thinking, she gave him a quick kiss on the cheek.

Damian pulled back then glanced behind her. "You probably shouldn't have done that."

Mya turned to find Guy charging toward them. From the hard set of his jaw, he was furious.

She tilted her head. Why? Because she had hugged her friend?

"I should go." Damian left her and made his way back into the house. He intercepted Guy on the way back to the mansion, and the two men exchanged quick words before Guy continued striding toward her. Whatever Damian had said had done nothing to lessen his anger.

"What the hell are you doing out here?"

Her back drew up, and she was incensed at his nerve. "I was talking to my friend. What do you care?"

"That didn't look like talking."

"Why? Because I gave my friend a hug for making me feel better about my *husband* not paying me any attention?"

His gaze took on a hard glint. "Keep your damn voice down."

"What for?" she spat. "They're probably talking about us now. Especially after the way you chose to ignore me and gush over your ex-girlfriend. I guess I'm lucky you even remembered I was here!"

"Believe me, you're hard to ignore," he barked. "Not when I have to hear about how great you and Damian danced together all night."

Mya gaped at him. "Are you jealous of Damian?"

The muscles in his jaw flexed. They said jealousy was a sign of caring, but she wondered if Guy's jealous anger had little to do with her and more to do with his pride and ego.

"Are you trying to make me?"

"Of course not. But it would be nice to know if you actually still cared about me. If you still wanted me the way I want you."

She searched his face, trying to figure out what he was thinking, waiting for him to say something—anything—that would give her some kind of assurance that he did care. But like a stubborn ass, he remained silent. Her irritation rose up a notch.

"So you don't want me, *and* you don't want anyone else to want me. Is that it?"

Anger flared in his eyes. "Remember where we are, Mya. This isn't some big city where you can sleep around with whoever you want. People are always watching and gossiping. We're supposed to be a happy couple, so fucking act like it."

Her back drew up. How dare he talk to her like that? And did he really expect her to pretend they were happy? Did other people's thoughts of them matter more to him than actually fixing their relationship?

Mya blew out a breath in disgust. "Screw this. I'm not pretending anything. You either put in some effort to make us happy, or I'll just find someone who wants, and will *appreciate*, my company."

She pushed past him and hurried toward the house, still shaking from her outburst. They had never fought like this, and she didn't know where her veiled threat would lead, but she wouldn't take it back.

"Mya!"

She flinched at his forceful shout but didn't stop. He caught up with her, his large hand snaking around her arm and jerking her to a stop.

"Get back here," he said through clenched teeth.

"Let go of me, Guy."

"I'm still talking to you, damn it." His grip around her arm was like a manacle. "There are a lot of people in there who have enough shit to say about us. Stop giving them more."

"What do you care? As far as everyone knows we're still just dating, right?"

She tried to pull out of his grasp. He tightened his hold.

"Pretend marriage or not, I'm not going to sit back and let you fuck around on me. Do you hear me?"

She could feel the rising anger pulsing through him. Pain shot up her arm and she flinched.

"Guy, you're hurting me!"

He let go of her as if he'd just been burned, and she stumbled back from the sudden release. She rubbed her arm, trying to ease the lingering sting.

"What's the matter with you? I have no intention of sleeping around. It's *you* that I want, *you jackass*. How many times do I have to tell you that?"

He turned away from her and ran his hand through his hair. She could sense his frustration and indecision, and it nearly broke her heart.

"It would be so much easier if you would just stop fighting it and forgive me already."

He whipped his head around to face her, and his face was a hard, guarded mask. "Let's get one thing clear so you know where we stand. What we have is a temporary arrangement. You need a place to stay, and I need you around long enough to get Warren to stop shoving his daughter my way. That is it."

She stared at him blankly, reeling from his cold words. What little bubble of hope she had held for them was quickly starting to fizzle out.

"So you're just using me?"

His eyes were as flat as his tone. "We're using each other."

Eight

"WHERE DO YOU WANT THIS, Gloria?"

"Oh, that can also go in the donation bin," she said, pushing back her eyeglasses. "I haven't been able to sell that in two years. I think frills are officially out of style."

Mya studied the garment, not sure when it had ever been back in style. She dropped the frilly dark blue garment in the box and moved on to the next piece of clothing.

They were almost done getting the back room of the boutique shop cleared to make room for her soap-making station. It was an idea that Mya had been entertaining for a while now. The thought of starting her own business selling homemade body soaps and moisturizers had initially freaked her out. She had no training in managing anything, and no patience to sit through a four-year degree to learn. But once she got used to the idea, the dream began to grow.

Luckily, confiding in Gloria about her plans had sparked a brilliant arrangement between them. Mya would work part-time with Gloria at the boutique, learning the ropes and shadowing her. The other half of Mya's time would be spent building her products and setting up her online store. As much as she loved the people of Cedar Bend, she knew she would have more success selling her products to a larger crowd.

"Mya, does this look familiar?"

She glanced at the frilly pink dress and laughed. "Oh my gosh! I can't believe you still have that." Mya took the old dress from Gloria and held it up. "And I can't believe Daddy let me wear this for a whole year."

Gloria shook her head, chuckling. "And if I hadn't dragged you in here, you probably would have gone another year wearing it."

Mya smiled at the thought. At the sage old age of six, she had declared herself a "princess," and this had been her royal gown—a shimmery pink dress with lots of frills. Apparently her dad had seen nothing wrong with that. Having been made a single parent after her mother remarried and moved back to England, her dad had barely survived that first year on his own. Fortunately, with Gloria's interference—and her wide selection of prettier dresses—Mya had eventually let go of her "princess dress."

"Poor Daddy. I was such a handful."

Gloria snickered. "What do you want to do with it? Donation?"

Mya stared at the dress again and smiled faintly. The old garb held lots of happy memories, and she imagined her little girl wearing it someday. A little girl that looked like her and Guy. She didn't have a wedding dress to pass down to her future daughter, so this would have to do…

"I think I'll keep it."

Mya folded the garment and placed it in her "keeper" pile. Once she had the discarded and unwanted items separated, she and Gloria began shoving the heavy crates to the front of the store. They were both sweating by the time they were done moving the last of them.

"Who knew clothes would be so heavy."

Gloria huffed and dabbed at the sweat at her temples with the heel of her hand. "Oh, I had an idea. But years in this business have built my strength, or else I would never get anything done around here."

"I don't know how you do it," Mya muttered, shrugging off her thin cardigan. She tossed the light sweater on the table and rested her hand on her hip.

"Years of practice, honey. I'm just glad we're done. Lunch break?"

"Yes!"

Gloria chuckled at her enthusiasm. "I need to run out later, but—"

Her words were abruptly cut off and Mya turned to her. Gloria's usually warm brown eyes were sharp with awareness as she stared intently at her shoulder.

Mya remembered the tattoo there—undoubtedly peeking through the straps of her tank top—and stifled a groan. She normally forgot it was there until someone stared at it. Not that she regretted the tattoo, but Gloria had always been like a surrogate mother to her. Mya didn't want to hear a lecture on the dangers or immorality of body defacement. She had gotten enough of that talk from her actual mother and stepfather.

But Gloria wasn't looking at her shoulder. She was staring intently at her arm, her brow deeply furrowed. Mya held her breath and waited for the question.

The bruise that had formed there wasn't as bad as Gloria's expression would make it seem, and to Mya's relief, she didn't ask about it.

Instead, Gloria said briskly, "Nice tattoo."

"You approve?"

The corner of her lips kicked up. She turned, pulled up the back of her shirt, and exposed the small butterfly on her lower back. Mya could only gape at it.

"Gloria! You have a tramp stamp?"

"Hey, I was young once too… And maybe just a little wild."

Mya laughed. "Does Guy know about this?" She remembered the disapproving look he'd given her when he'd seen her ink. At least Gloria's wasn't visible to the general public.

"He doesn't, and I suspect he would collapse in shock if he did."

They both snorted, finding it hard to imagine Guy collapsing over anything.

In the back room, they finally settled down to lunch and ate the simple meal Gloria had packed. Because the store was usually slow on Sundays, Gloria decided to close it for the day while they completed their redecoration. Now that Mya was coming back to help, they were planning other exciting changes for the shop, some of which included a section to display her body care products and a separate area for more craft and sewing classes.

"So how are you and Guy getting along lately?"

Mya shrugged, concentrating on her lunch. "Things could be better."

"What's going on?"

Mya didn't want to lie to her, but neither did she want the added scrutiny on their already strained relationship. Things were difficult enough without Gloria's well-intentioned interference.

"Nothing. We just got into it last night at Eric's party and things have been a bit tense."

When Gloria glanced at her arm again, Mya shifted uncomfortably. She reached for her light sweater and slipped it on.

"What was the fight about?"

"It was stupid, really."

Mya couldn't even pinpoint what had set him off in the first place. She could only guess that he'd thought she'd set out to make him jealous, but that certainly had not been the case. All she had wanted from him last night was his attention. Making him jealous was not how she wanted to get it.

"You know how stubborn Guy can be. I don't know where he gets it, but just give him some time."

Mya nodded, but what he'd said last night had begun planting doubts in her heart about them. Every time she thought they were making progress, he would close up on her. Yet why hadn't he sought out a divorce? A part of her still believed he wanted them to be together. She just needed to show him how serious she was about making their relationship work.

"I really wish I knew what to say to get him to forgive me already."

Gloria patted her hand. "Maybe there's nothing you can say," she muttered. "Just give him time. He'll come around. Then you'll get married and live happily ever after."

Mya shifted in her seat again, a strained chuckle coming out of her at Gloria's teasing. They were already married, but they certainly weren't happy.

She wanted nothing more than to make their marriage public—at the very least, tell Gloria. Maybe if everyone knew, it would finally start to feel real to her. Because the sad truth was that their marriage had never felt real—not then and certainly not now.

Guy looked up from the reports he was reviewing when his mother burst into his office. She didn't stop until she was standing beside his desk, peering down at him from behind her gold-framed eyeglasses. Her lips were set in hard lines. This was bad.

"Ma, what—"

"Did you do that to her?"

"Do what? To who?"

Her eyes narrowed. "Here, let me jog your memory." In a blur, her hand lashed out and smacked him on the side of the head.

"Ma!" He frowned, rubbing his head. "What the hell was that for?"

She said nothing. Just stood there, pursing her red lips and planting her hands on her hips. He endured the silence for a while longer, determined to wait her out— glare for glare.

In the end, she won.

With a weary sigh, Guy threw his pen down on the desk and leaned back in his seat. "Ma, I don't have time to get into it with you today. I have a lot of work—"

"Have I ever laid my hands on you in anger when you were a kid?"

"What?"

"Have I?"

"No. Not until today, anyway," he muttered bitterly, absently rubbing the still-tender spot on his head.

"Have you ever seen me let a man raise his voice to me, much less his hands, since your father?"

"No, because I wouldn't let that happen."

"And I won't let you go on abusing Mya."

Guy straightened in his seat. "What are you talking about?"

"Did you or did you not put that bruise on her arm?"

He stared at his mother blankly until her words finally registered. "Shit," he muttered, running his hand over his face.

He remembered how angry he'd been with Mya last night, but he hadn't realized he'd been so rough. He'd never been jealous in his life, but seeing Mya in the arms of another man—even if it was a good friend of his— had brought up so many insecurities in him.

"I raised you better than that, Guy. I won't tolerate you getting violent with her."

"Ma—"

"If Marvin could see how you're treating his daughter, he would rise from his grave and beat the crap out of you. And I would let him!"

His mother gave him a glare that made him feel smaller than his six-two frame. It was the same look she'd given him when he was ten and had been suspended for breaking Cody Fischer's nose. He'd felt like shit then. Not because he'd broken the boy's nose—the son-of-a-bitch deserved it for talking about his mother—but that one look had said how disappointed she was with him, and Guy never wanted to see that look on her face again.

He blew out a breath. "Ma, would you settle down? I didn't mean to hurt her."

"What you *meant* to do doesn't matter. We're talking about what you did, and I'm very disappointed in you right now."

Heat rose to his cheeks. For the first time in his adult life, he was thoroughly contrite. He didn't think he could feel any more like shit than he did now.

"I'm sorry—"

"I don't want to hear it," she snapped, waving his words away. "I'm not the one who needs your apology. You make this right, and you do it today!"

With that, his mother stormed out of his office.

Guy stared after her. He'd never seen her so upset, but he couldn't blame her. Part of the reason she and his father had split was because of the man's temper.

And he was appalled at his own explosive temper.

He'd never hurt a woman before, and no matter how angry he was at Mya, he would never intentionally harm her.

Guy reached for the phone then placed it back down. What would he say? He obviously needed to apologize, but he needed to do it in person.

Unfortunately, it was late when Guy left the station. The entire ride home, he thought of what he would say to her.

The house was dark when he pulled up beside her car in the driveway. Guy made his way into his bedroom and stopped just outside the bathroom door. The scent of her soap—the one he loved so much—filled the room. The sweet smell brought back so many memories of him nuzzling her smooth neck, her arms wrapped firmly around him.

His body instantly reacted to the long-ago memory of having her in his arms and making love to her for the first time. She had been warm and smelled just as sweet then...

Guy shook the memory away and raised his hand to the door. Just as he was about to knock, a loud shriek came from inside. His heart dropped, and he practically kicked the door in.

"Mya!"

She shrieked again, her hand flying to her throat.

"Guy! You scared me."

His hand was still on the doorknob as he quickly scanned her. "You screamed."

She cradled her fist in her other hand. "I caught my finger in the drawer. That's all."

"Oh."

Suddenly he realized she had only a towel wrapped around her. A thick, soft pink one that came down just to her knees. Her smooth brown skin still glistened with evidence of her shower.

Moving without much thought, Guy came fully into the bathroom and stood directly in front of her.

She quietly regarded him with large brown eyes, and at that moment, he was lost in their depth. She didn't bother concealing her love and desire as she stared up at him. That was what he loved most about her—the way she didn't conceal her affections. Even now, she was an open book with her feelings.

Why couldn't she be open with him that night?

Guy glanced away from her, breaking the spell that threatened to undo his resolve. It was then he saw the bruises on her arm. The dark discoloration staining her skin left him sick to his stomach.

"I did that?" He shook his head. "I shouldn't have grabbed you like that."

She glanced down at her arm then back up at him. "No, you shouldn't have. But it doesn't hurt. I just bruise easily sometimes."

"I'm sorry. I didn't mean to do that."

"I know you didn't." She came closer to him, placing her palm on his abdomen. "But thank you for apologizing."

His gut clenched from the light touch, and he inhaled sharply, taking in her hypnotic smell. Nothing he did could ever rid him of his need for her. But the last thing he wanted to do was complicate things between them.

With more difficulty than he expected, he pulled away from her. Disappointment flashed in her beautiful eyes, and it took everything he had not to give in to what they both wanted.

Nine

MYA RUSHED INTO THE HOUSE, juggling the bag of groceries while trying to get to her ringing cell phone. She managed to make it to the kitchen—and her phone—before the caller hung up.

"Hello."

The number had come up "unavailable," but she was hoping it was Guy calling to wish her a happy Valentine's Day.

"Zamya, honey, were you running?"

Mya's shoulders fell. Not that she didn't want to speak to her mother, but there was one person she'd been hoping to hear from all day, and he hadn't even bothered to text her. Since that night he apologized, things had been better between them. It wasn't *great*, certainly not where she wanted them to be—and not with him still sleeping in the guest room—but at least he wasn't going out of his way to avoid her.

"Hi, Mum."

"Hello, honey. Happy Valentine's day."

Mya couldn't help but smile. "Thanks, Mum, but I can't believe you called me at your hour just to tell me that." She glanced at the clock on the wall. "It's almost midnight where you are."

"I know, but I wanted to be sure I called you before it was too late. I would have called earlier, but Jeffrey took me out on the most fabulous day trip…"

Mya listened to her mother's fluid British accent as she went on about the wonderfulness that was her second husband. Not that Mya had anything against the man—he did treat her mother like a queen—but as a wealthy African diplomat, he tended to be highly conservative and a bit arrogant. Maybe she wouldn't mind him so much if her mother didn't feel compelled to constantly talk about his wonderful qualities and how she, as her only daughter, needed to be less "combative."

In her opinion, defending her choice to live her life the way she wanted and not attend college didn't constitute being confrontational. But, apparently, the more Mya rejected their "advice," the more defensive— and rebellious—she was behaving.

And that part was true.

Her tattoo was a result of that rebellion. Her mother and stepfather may not have approved, but the small artwork served as a reminder to rid herself of the emotional restraints she had carried with her to England—and give herself permission to feel again.

After fifteen minutes of her mother's story, Mya cut her off.

"Sounds like you had a great time, Mum, but I really have to go. Guy will be home soon and I want to make dinner for him tonight."

"What? You mean he's not taking you out? But it's Valentine's Day."

Mya was more than aware. Today wasn't just a holiday for them. It meant so much more. At least it had once.

Mya shook the thought away. She had promised herself she wouldn't let their recent tension change her plans. She was going to make tonight special and try to close the gap that seemed to be expanding between them.

"Dinner at home with my—" *Husband.* Mya caught the word before it slipped out. "—my Guy is all I need to celebrate Valentine's Day."

Her mother huffed, but let the topic drop. "Well, I won't keep you, then. I just wanted to let you know that a letter from Cambridge came for you."

The excitement in her mother's voice filled Mya with guilt. She had only applied to the university to appease her mother and had no intention of returning to England, much less going to school there.

"Really?" Mya said with forced interest. "What did it say?"

"I didn't open it, of course. Though I wanted to! But I thought we could open it together. Over the phone, I mean."

"Uh, why don't we do it some other night," Mya said. "It's already late for you and I have so much on my mind already."

"But—"

"Please, Mum. I really don't want to hear bad news tonight."

It wasn't a complete lie. Bad news would be finding out that she was accepted into the prestigious university—then having to tell her mother that she wasn't going.

"Okay, honey. We'll open it another night."

Relieved, Mya said a quick goodbye then pushed all thoughts of England and school aside. With only an hour before Guy got home, she rushed to prepare their meal.

An hour was all the time she needed.

By the time she finished setting up the table, she only had a few minutes to admire her picture-perfect set up before she hurried through her shower and changed into her favorite red dress.

But another hour passed and still no Guy.

Mya debated whether to call him. It was a little after seven. On Valentine's Day. He should be home by now.

She stared at her phone for what seemed like an eternity then grabbed it. Before she could talk herself out of it, she sent him a text.

Hey. When will you be home?

She waited several minutes before he finally responded.

Late.

Mya blew out a frustrated breath and jabbed in her next message with more force than she wanted.

How late?

This time she waited much longer for his response, and for a moment she thought he wouldn't answer. When her cell phone vibrated, she snatched it from the table.

Don't wait up.

That was all he wrote, and she immediately thought the worst. Was he with another woman? It had been over a week since she'd come back and he had made no attempts to touch her, though she could see the desire burning in his eyes.

She started another message.

Do you know what today is?

She instantly deleted it. He had to know. It was more than just Valentine's Day. It was the anniversary of the first time he told her he loved her—and promised his love was forever.

Unconsciously, her fingers came up to her neck and she touched the small jewel nestled at her throat. As beautiful as the necklace was, he had given her something far greater.

His heart.

Of course he wasn't with another woman.

Mya shook her head at even having the thought. He would never break his vow to her like that. And she didn't believe in her heart he had given up on their marriage.

After blowing out the candles, she grabbed the bottle of wine from the table. She made her way to the living room and turned on the television. Settling into the large couch, Mya grabbed the warm afghan and draped it across her legs.

So much for her happy Valentine's Day.

Guy walked into the house to find the lights turned low. It was late, and he imagined Mya was already in bed.

He unbuttoned his shirt on his way to the guest room, but froze when he passed the dining room. On the table was a dinner set up for two, with a small bouquet of roses and tall candle in the center. The wick was burned at the end and the meal was virtually untouched.

What the hell...

The date suddenly dawned on him and Guy leaned against the wall, feeling like a complete ass. It was Valentine's Day.

He knew what today meant to her. It had meant the same to him once. On their first Valentine's together, he had taken her to Promise Lane and given her the necklace—and his promise to love and protect her always. That was the first time he'd told another woman, other than his mother, that he loved her.

With a small curse, Guy pushed away from the wall and went searching for her. She wasn't in any of the bedrooms, and a slow panic began to build in him.

It immediately fell away when he found her in the den, curled up on the sofa. An empty glass and a half-empty bottle of wine was on the center table. An infomercial for tabletop grills played in the background, and she slept through it all. She looked vulnerable and small curled on the couch like that, like someone who needed caring and protecting. But that was a bad habit he needed to break. She wasn't a kid anymore, and she certainly wasn't weak.

Guy made his way to the sofa and stared down at her a moment longer. Even asleep, she was breathtaking. He could see evidence of the painstaking steps she had taken with her appearance tonight.

With a small sigh, Guy carefully pulled back the throw blanket and gathered her in his arms. He lifted her high against his chest, and she murmured but didn't wake. Instead, she cuddled closer and released a soft sigh, her breath tickling the side of his face.

Sharp desire pierced through him and his grip involuntarily tightened around her. He imagined her naked body pressed against his, her breath teasing his throat, while he was deep inside her. His shaft grew unbearably full, and he clenched his jaw against the intense need building in him.

Guy scoffed. He only had himself to blame for his discomfort. Apparently, she couldn't even breathe without giving him a hard-on.

When he finally reached his bedroom, he carefully laid her on the bed and pulled the covers over her.

"Guy?"

He stilled. "Yeah?"

She propped herself up and looked around the dark room. "Where… What time is it?"

"It's late. You fell asleep. I'm just putting you to bed."

She sat up and brushed the loose strands of her hair behind her ear. "You missed dinner."

Guilt once again seared through him. "You shouldn't have gone through the trouble."

"It's—was Valentine's Day."

"I know."

"So you stayed out all night on purpose?"

"No, I was working. I told you I would be late."

"What was so important you couldn't come home until" —she glanced at the clock on the nightstand— "*midnight?*"

"I said I was at work, Mya. I'm not about to itemize every step of my day with you."

He turned to leave, but she grabbed his hand. He stopped but didn't pull away from her.

"Guy, wait. I don't want us to fight."

She tugged on his hand until he came down on the bed. He knew he should turn and walk out now, but he was powerless against her gentle urging.

"I just wanted us to have tonight."

She rested her hand on his chest and he was lost from the light touch, swept away by the overwhelming tide of his desires. He sat frozen for a millisecond as she fitted her lips against his. She was soft and warm and everything he had dreamed of having.

Wrapping his arms around her neck, he drew her to him and deepened the kiss. Her fingers clutched at his shirt as he moved his lips over hers, familiarizing himself with the taste and feel of her again.

Yet it still wasn't enough.

Guy jerked off her dress, and only when he felt her soft, smooth skin beneath his fingers did his anxiety ease. He trailed his lips down the column of her throat, savoring its smooth texture, her soft moans nearly sending him over the edge. He had gone too long without her, and there was nothing that could pry him out of her arms.

Not tonight.

With frenzied movements, they stripped off the rest of their clothing. They were skin to skin within a matter of minutes. Her small, plump breasts pushed against his chest, and for a moment he held her to him, committing every sensation to memory.

God, I missed you.

When she began to kiss along his neck and jaw, he lost what little hold he had on his self-control. At that moment, nothing mattered but being inside her and reclaiming the passion, the love they had once shared.

Guy fell over her on the bed and settled himself between her thighs. He brought his lips down to hers as he began to slowly push into her. She was unbelievably tight, and he gritted his teeth against the incredible sensation. The soft pulsing of her warm channel around his shaft nearly drove him over the edge.

"Relax, baby," he murmured, still gliding into her with excruciating care.

She dug her fingers into his shoulders as he continued to bury himself in her, but he was the one wired to break. He wanted to unleash all the pent-up desire he held, but his fear of hurting her kept him from pounding into her.

She wrapped her arms around his neck and gradually lifted her hips against him. A harsh groan tore through him and he sank deeper into her.

In the cover of night, he lost himself in the moment, making up for those many nights he'd burned for her. And it was as exquisite as he remembered.

When her soft cries echoed through the dark room, he covered her mouth with his and greedily took everything she had to give before he found his own release.

The next morning, Mya woke to find herself alone in bed.

She rolled onto her back and stretched, the tender pulling between her legs a delicious reminder of last night, which had been…

She had no words for it.

It had been more intense than their first night together. There was no way he could make love to her the way he had last night and pretend as if he didn't love her. For the first time since she'd been back, Mya felt more than a glimmer of hope for them.

The shower in the connecting bathroom suddenly came on. She gingerly got out of bed and slipped on a pair of panties and her favorite sleep shirt. She was relieved and a bit anxious that he hadn't left before they had a chance to see each other yet. Last night was exactly what they needed, and she could only hope that he felt the same way.

Mya made her way to the kitchen, and her first stop was at the coffee maker. She threw out the dinner left out from last night and began making breakfast. Years of preparing meals for her and her dad made the task quick and easy. She fell into a comfortable routine as she prepared a simple meal of scrambled eggs, sausage, and cheesy grits.

By the time Guy made his way into the kitchen, breakfast was on the table. But he said nothing as he went to the cabinet and took down a mug.

She didn't want things to be awkward between them, so she turned and forced cheerfulness into her voice.

"Good morning."

"Morning," he said over his shoulder.

"Are you hungry?"

"Not really."

"Well, you should eat anyway. Here, I fixed you a plate."

To her relief, he didn't argue. He sat down at the table and started in on his meal. She fell into the seat across from him, acutely aware that she had nothing on underneath her simple nightshirt, besides panties. She needed to get ready for work herself, but she didn't want to miss this opportunity to spend a little more time with him.

They ate in silence—a silence that had so many questions and unsaid words hovering between them.

When Mya couldn't take the quiet any longer, she finally blurted, "Will you be working late again tonight?"

"Not if I can help it," he muttered, not looking up at her.

"Good. Then what would you like for dinner tonight?"

He placed his fork down and leaned back in his seat, studying her. She shifted under his close scrutiny then tensed, sensing an excuse—or refusal to have dinner at home with her—coming.

"Mya—"

"I cooked what chicken we had left," she cut in. "But I can make a casserole or stew."

"Mya, I don't want you to make dinner."

She tried to mask her disappointment. "Why not?"

"Because the mayor's having a function tonight and he invited me to come."

"Oh."

"Can you be ready by seven?"

Her head jerked up in surprise. "You want me to come?"

"Do you want to?"

"Yes, of course."

He visibly relaxed and gave her a curt nod. Then suddenly he leaned forward in his seat, his brow furrowed as if he were carefully weighing his next words. "About last night…"

"What about it?"

"It was——"

"Nice," she finished for him.

He cocked a brow and his lips quirked up slightly. "Only nice?"

Her cheeks warmed. Thoughts of last night flooded her, reminding her just how incredible they had been together. To her mortification, her nipples grew taut and pushed against her thin shirt, craving his touch.

"You know what I mean. It was amazing and I have no regrets."

He stared at her searchingly. "Neither do I. But it's going to complicate things."

"No, it won't," she said. Before he could say anything else, she rose and began gathering their dishes.

"Leave it," he said. "I'll put it in the dishwasher."

"Thanks." She wanted to kiss him before she left but was suddenly feeling awkward again. "I should go get ready. Gloria will never let me hear the end of it if I open the shop even five minutes late."

She walked past him, regretting that lost moment of intimacy, but was surprised when he grabbed her hand and pulled her to a stop.

"I'm sorry about last night. For missing dinner."

She smiled, warmed by the unexpected apology. Tossing her pride and uncertainty aside, she leaned down and kissed him. What should have been a quick peck became a long, lingering kiss. He cupped the back of her neck and she braced herself against his shoulders.

His hands slid under her shirt and he slowly dragged her panties down her legs.

"Guy?" she breathed. "What are you doing?"

"You said last night was *nice*." He pushed their dishes aside and pulled her down on the edge of the breakfast table. "I need to make up for that."

Mya held her breath as he pushed her down on the table and lifted her legs high. When his mouth covered her throbbing flesh, she gasped and grabbed his head. His tongue moved over her with expert skill, licking and stroking her with a gentle caress that left her panting. She lifted her hips, eager to take more of his teasing mouth.

With a throaty sigh, she fell back on the table and held on to him, not sure if she wanted to take more of his gentle assault or push him away. In the end, he decided for her. Looping his arms around her thighs, he pulled her to him and held her still. She tried yet failed to hold back her cries of pleasure.

His skilled mouth move voraciously over her sensitive flesh and her body caved under the delicious pressure. With a soft scream, she tightened her legs around his head and came with an intensity that bordered on pain.

She was certain the whole town had heard her moans of release.

Her entire body still shook as ripples of pleasure moved over her. With a few soothing laps of his tongue, he eased her back to reality. When she found the strength, she opened her eyes to find him staring down at her, his green eyes bright with unspent desire. Her quivering thighs hung like soft noodles over the table. Moving over her, he kissed her deeply and without restraint.

"Now *that*," she panted into his mouth, "was incredible."

Ten

GUY WAS IMPATIENT TO LEAVE.

Not that Warren's dinner party was dull. It was as conservative as he expected, but had certainly turned up a crowd. Guy, however, was eager to be back home with Mya. He couldn't stop thinking about her—or last night.

She had been in the forefront of his thoughts all day. Making love to her again had bulldozed right through his wall of resolve. What little remained standing had been crushed that morning.

Guy's lips curved at the vivid memory. Like he'd told her that morning, he had no regrets. She was the love of his life, and last night had not only reminded him of that, it cemented it.

It was a terrifying feeling, opening himself up to her again, exposing himself to potential heartbreak again, but he couldn't pretend as if he hadn't felt something last night. Not after what they shared.

After a few more minutes of polite conversation with a group of Warren's ardent supporters, Guy went in search of Mya. He had put in enough time here.

The mayor's mansion wasn't as large as the Bensons' but it was large enough to hold a sizeable crowd and turned what should have been a dinner party into a social gathering.

Guy came up to where she stood chatting with the same group of women he'd left her with earlier. When he found his opening, he leaned down and asked close to her ear, "Are you ready to go?"

She turned to him and her courteous smile instantly fell away. Her gaze fell to his lips and took on that familiar warm glow, as if she sensed the burning need he tried to suppress.

Needing the contact, he took her hand and gave it a squeeze. It was about time he reconciled with his wife properly.

"Let's go."

She nodded, and after they said their goodbyes, he led them through the crowd of people.

"Guy, slow down."

Slowing his steps, he glanced back at her and caught a glimpse of her high heels. She was once again dressed stylishly, causing a stir not just in him. But she could have been in her old sleep shirt and he would have found her as irresistible as he did now.

When they were finally away from prying eyes, Guy stopped and pulled her into a deep kiss. It took only a moment for her to melt into his embrace. But before he could lose himself in her seductive taste, he pulled away. She blinked, still holding on to his biceps.

"What was that for?"

He shrugged, running the pad of his thumb along her jaw line. "No reason. Just making up for lost time."

Her eyes moved over his searchingly. "Does that mean you finally forgive me?"

He continued to savor the feel of her soft skin as he thought seriously about her question. The sudden realization that he did—that he no longer held any more of the anger and resentment—was liberating. Almost freeing. He had his woman back and he wouldn't waste any more time holding on to past mistakes.

"I do love you, Guy. You don't have to say the words back. I just want you to know that I do."

I love you too.

But he wasn't prepared to say the words. Not yet. What he felt for her left him feeling too raw and exposed. Instead, he brought his finger under her chin and lifted her face to his.

"Don't ever leave me again."

"Never."

He brushed his lips against hers. The kiss they shared was light and sweet—until she looped her arms around his neck and deepened the kiss.

"Sorry to interrupt."

Guy stifled a groan and turned to the mayor.

"Guy, can I have a word with you?"

"Mya and I were just heading out."

Warren glanced from him to Mya, his expression more guarded than usual. "I just need a few minutes of your time. In private."

"Can it wait until Monday?"

Warren's mouth was set in a grim line. "I'm afraid it can't."

Mya patted his hand before pulling away. "It's okay." Then added in a hushed tone, "I need to pee, anyway."

Guy followed the mayor into his office, apprehension filling his gut like a pack of lodestones.

"Have a seat."

Guy watched the mayor head to his minibar and pour himself a drink. What the hell was going on?

"Are you a scotch man, Guy?"

"Not particularly."

Guy watched as the man downed his drink then pour himself another. Warren nodded toward the sofa behind him as he fell into the seat across.

"Sit."

Guy reluctantly fell into the seat. "Warren, what is it?"

The mayor downed his drink and placed the glass on the table. "You understand how important this election is to me, right? I have a lot that I'd still like to accomplish, and programs that I'd like to launch that will preserve the integrity and values of our town."

Guy frowned, irritated to be having this conversation with the man again. "With all due respect, Warren, but that's the same message you've run your last two campaigns on. Not much of what you promised has been delivered in your two terms as mayor. An endorsement from me won't do you any good until the town starts to see real progress."

"Thank you for your candor, but an endorsement isn't why I wanted to speak with you tonight. I actually need something greater than that."

"Like what?"

"A situation has developed that may hurt my chances at re-election, and I need to get in front of it before it does irreparable damage to my campaign."

"What is it you need from me?"

Warren leaned forward in his seat. "I'm going to cut to the chase. I need you to marry Sophie."

Guy could only stare at the older man, stunned and unsure he'd heard him correctly. "Excuse me?"

"It'll all be temporary. Until we get through this election. Then we can arrange for a quick and quiet annulment."

"Why marriage?" Guy asked, still trying to process the mayor's bizarre request. He'd had very little interaction with Sophia Powers and didn't know much about her other than she was the youngest of Warren's three girls. "Isn't there another option?"

"I'm afraid not. Besides, Eric Benson's wedding has been the talk of the town. Wouldn't hurt to give them another one. I get a bump in the polls and find a temporary fix for this problem."

"And what problem is that?"

"I need to know if I have your support before I go into any detail."

Guy stared at him, incredulous. "We're talking about marriage here, Warren. Not some endorsement or campaign contribution."

He shrugged. "Many may not agree, but politics is like a marriage, and marriage is dirty business. Complete with all the contracts and commitments."

"For me, marriage is bigger than that."

Warren cocked a brow. "I didn't know you were so sentimental."

Guy clenched his jaw. The mayor could believe whatever he wanted, but marriage was about making a commitment to the woman he loved—the woman he planned to have children with and grow old with.

Mya was that woman. And she was his wife.

"I can't marry your daughter."

Warren's eyes were shrewd. "That's it? You're not even going to hear what I'll offer you if you go through with this?"

Son-of-a-bitch.

Guy shouldn't have been surprised by this ploy, but he was disgusted the man thought he would enter into such an absurd arrangement just for a promotion.

"Whatever you have to offer won't change anything, Warren. I can't marry your daughter."

"Why not?"

"I think the real question is why *me?*"

"Let's just say you're the only man I trust to act...honorably and with discretion toward my daughter."

Guy scoffed, not buying his bullshit. "No, you thought I'd be desperate enough for the promotion to agree to some sham marriage."

The mayor shrugged. "I wouldn't call it desperate, but you want something that I can give you. In turn, I'm asking for this favor."

Guy rose from his seat. He was done with this conversation. It wouldn't amount to anything, anyway, since he was already married and he had every intention of staying that way.

"The answer is still no. I'm sure you'll find someone more suitable to take your daughter off your hands." He started toward the door and froze at the mayor's next words.

"There's a sizeable raise that could come with that promotion, Guy. And I'm sure we can find some money in the budget to make sure you and your deputies have all that you need."

"I won't be manipulated," Guy snapped.

Warren got to his feet. "Don't let your feelings for Miss Daniels get in the way of your better judgment."

"Keep her out of this."

The mayor's eyes widened at the vehemence in his voice. "Look, I can see how strongly you feel for her, but you're looking at this all wrong. Marrying Sophie would be strictly a business arrangement. Temporary at that. And don't you want the best for your deputies?"

"I do, but I won't accomplish that by letting you worm your way back into office."

Something cold flashed in Warren's eyes before he quickly masked it. "Did it ever occur to you that maybe this is really about helping my daughter?"

"I'm sure whatever your reason, it has everything to do with you and your damn campaign."

"Remember, your position as sheriff is only temporary. I would hate to start actively looking for a more permanent one."

Guy's jaw clenched as he held on to his temper. "I'm not going to be bullied into marrying your daughter, so save it. Besides, you said it best. Making my position permanent could only help you in this election. Either way, I get to keep my job, so do whatever the hell you want."

Warren's lips curved in a mirthless smile. "We have nine months until the election, Guy. A lot of good could come from my office to your department in that amount of time. Why don't you take this weekend to think about it? We'll touch base on Monday."

Guy shook his head. "I don't need to think about it. The answer is, and will always be, *no*."

Warren fixed him with a level glare. "You would sacrifice everything I'm offering for one woman. You love her that much?"

"Yes. I do."

"Then I was wrong about you. You're weaker than I thought."

Mya shifted above him, her naked body moving sleepily over his.

Guy absently ran his hand along the smooth dip of her waist and down the curve of her hips.

She shifted again then lifted her head from his shoulder. "Guy? You're still awake?"

"Just thinking, babe. Go back to sleep."

She ignored him, and instead ran the back of her fingers along the short, stiff hairs budding at his jaw. "What are you thinking about?"

He wrapped his arms around her and held her close. It was late and they both were exhausted. Just an hour ago they had been locked in a fiery embrace, his body making up for lost time, yet still unable to get enough of her. But that wasn't what kept him up tonight.

"You're thinking about the talk you had with the mayor tonight?"

"It is that obvious?"

"Yes. You had the same frown on your face after you talked with him. Like you do now." She brought a finger to his forehead and began to smooth it over his furrowed brow. "Was it about his daughter?"

"What makes you say that?" he asked, keeping his voice neutral.

"You mentioned the other night that the mayor was throwing his daughter your way. I'm not surprised. You're a great catch, Guy. I'm not surprised that he wants you dating his daughter."

Guy bit back a snide remark about the mayor. The man's inability to see anything beyond his own self-interest and greed was staggering.

"Have you?"

Guy brows pulled together. "Have I what?"

"Dated anyone while we were…"

"Separated?" he finished for her.

She nodded, but above him, her body was rigid.

"You shouldn't ask questions you don't really want to know the answer to," he said quietly.

"Does that mean you have?"

He sighed. It meant that he didn't want to know. If she had gotten involved with another man while they were separated, he didn't think he could handle it. Hell, just the thought drove him crazy. He was content with the way things were going between them. He didn't want anything to disrupt that.

"You can tell me, Guy. I won't like it, but I won't be mad." There was a tension in her that was hard to ignore.

"Then why does it matter? I don't know about you, but I don't want to hash over what or who we did while we weren't together."

Her next words were clear and direct. "Guy, I didn't date or sleep with anyone while I was away. Meeting someone else wasn't why I left."

Though her confession eased some of his tension, it gave him little comfort because whether she wanted to admit it or not, she had left to get away from him. That was a harsh reality he couldn't forget.

"Why don't we just focus on right now and the future?"

"I just think our future will only be stronger if we're honest with each other. Even if it hurts."

She was right, of course. It was a lack of communication that had led to two wasted years.

"I haven't dated anyone else," he finally admitted.

The tension left her body and silence fell between them. She didn't ask for an explanation and he didn't offer one. Two years of celibacy hadn't been easy, but he'd still been married—and the woman he'd really wanted had been far out of his reach.

"So what did the mayor say tonight to upset you?"

"What makes you think he upset me?" he asked carefully.

"Because I know you, remember. And I know when you're upset. Now stop answering my questions with a question. You do that when you're trying to avoid being direct with me."

He chuckled and pressed his lips against her shoulder. "You know me too well."

"So…what did you guys talk about?"

How much did he tell her? He wanted to be honest with her in everything, but how could he tell her about the mayor's bizarre request?

"It's just a work thing. Nothing for you to worry about."

"You can still tell me, Guy. I'm your wife. We should talk about these things, especially when they keep you up at night."

My wife...

Those two words triggered something primitive in him. If that made him weak, so be it. Only she had the power to devastate him, but he had to trust that his love was safe with her. Warren Powers may think he was weak for loving his wife, but it was the opposite. Loving Mya made him feel as if he could conquer anything. He wouldn't let the mayor or his jaded views on love and marriage get in his head.

Guy glided his palm down her lush curves. "We *could* talk about how the mayor has cut the budget for the department and how difficult he's made it for all of us, but I'd rather focus on other things."

"Like what?" she murmured.

He moved his hand between her legs and slipped a finger inside her. "Like this."

Her soft sigh soon became a low moan, and his shaft stirred then hardened. He loved the sounds she made. Almost as much as he enjoyed the feel of her naked body pressing deliciously against him.

He flipped her on her back and entered her with one smooth stroke. Further thought of the cynical mayor vanished as Guy lost himself inside the woman he loved.

Eleven

"YOU'VE BEEN nothing but smiles all day today. I'm guessing you and Guy had a nice weekend?"

Mya looked up from the display she was arranging, her cheeks warming. "Yes, it was nice."

Actually, it had been better than nice.

She stifled a giggle, her body still humming from the endless pleasure he'd given her that weekend—and this morning.

Mya turned away from Gloria, hoping the older woman couldn't read the salacious thoughts running through her mind. This weekend had been Guy's one weekend off. They had spent it making up for lost time, and she loved every moment of it.

"I'm glad to see you smiling again. I was starting to worry you two wouldn't work things out."

"You were right, Gloria. He just needed time."

She would be patient. Things may not have returned completely to the way they once were, but the walls Guy had placed between them were slowly starting to crumble. He was kissing and touching her freely and the boyish grin she had fallen in love with so many years ago was back. This weekend alone had done a lot to strengthen their bond. It was just unfortunate that they wouldn't get another one like that until next month.

She sighed. "I only wish he didn't have to work so much. Maybe then we could spend more time together."

Gloria's nose scrunched. "You can thank the mayor for that. He's made budget cuts all over town. I understand there are times when we need to scale back, but I just don't understand how cutting funds at the hospital and police department helps us. Guy and the few deputies there have tried filling the gaps the best they can. Mike only took the job to help Guy out, but he's practically working for nothing."

From the little Guy had told her, Mya could finally understand why he worked so much. The past week Mya had seen him leave early and come home late. He did it without complaint—and practically every day. It hadn't been to avoid her, but to lessen the burden on his deputies.

"Can't we do something? Maybe write to his office?"

Gloria waved her hands away. "You know how these things go. I think everyone is just waiting out his term. At first, I was skeptical of Eric running for the position. He's so young, you know. But maybe he'll be the fresh air we need."

Mya hoped so. She liked Eric, but politics had a way of changing people. She remembered Mayor Powers had been a huge advocate for the safety of their town and the police officers who served it. Now he was stripping away the very protection the people of Cedar Bend had come to rely on?

Whatever the mayor had said to Guy the other night had set him on edge. Though she knew there was more than he was telling her, she didn't want to push. She would wait for him to confide in her when he was ready.

"Mya, did you hear me?"

She blinked and found Gloria staring at her. "Sorry. What did you say?"

"I'm heading to the CPA's office now. I might be a while. Will you be okay by yourself?"

"Yes, of course."

"All right. I'll try to be back soon, but if I'm not back before Sophie Powers comes to pick up her package, could you take care of it? I placed it under the counter."

Mya's eyes widened in surprise. Not that Gloria's boutique wasn't fashionable enough, but from what she remembered of the Powers women, they were what the British would call too *posh* for A Touch of Glam, despite the boutique name.

"Sophie Powers shops here?"

"Believe me, I was just as surprised as you. But this is her fifth order so far. She keeps this up, I just might have to forgive her father for being the snake he is." Gloria chuckled as she sailed out of the store.

Mya kept herself busy by untangling the necklaces she had found in the back. The store was quiet, as it had been for the past few days now. She could understand why Gloria couldn't afford to hire another clerk to help her around. With the amount of time she spent meeting with the bank or her accountant, she couldn't be trapped in the store all day.

Though Mya was happy she could relieve some of the burden, she was starting to think A Touch of Glam was going to need to make bigger changes aside from selling her homemade soaps if it was going to survive.

Putting Gloria's old computer beside the register to better use, Mya began surfing the web, looking for ideas from other stores that they could use around the boutique. She hadn't gotten far in her search when the bell above the front door chimed. She glanced up as Sophie Powers made her way toward the counter.

The petite brunette offered her a weak smile. "Where's Gloria?"

"She's at a meeting. She'll be back later."

"Oh. Okay." Her strained smile suddenly fell away. "Well, she said my order was ready."

"Yup, we have it right here." Mya reached beneath the counter and grabbed the small box. She tried to make small talk while she closed out the ticket, but the young woman appeared uninterested—or distracted. Mya tried not to let the woman's sour mood affect her.

"Would you like to try on the dress before you go? We have a changing room in the back."

Sophie chewed the bottom of her lip.

"If you try it on and find anything wrong, we can take care of it now so you won't have to come back in."

With a small sigh, she grabbed her package. "Sure. Fine. Where am I going?"

Mya led her to the back and got her set up. If Gloria didn't need the clientele, Mya wouldn't have bothered engaging the obviously uninterested woman.

About five minutes passed and yet there was no sign of Sophie. Mya had at least expected her to come out and ask for her opinion. When another five minutes passed, Mya made her way back toward the dressing area. If she wasn't mistaken, she would have sworn she heard sobbing coming from behind the curtain.

"Sophie, is everything okay?"

The crying stopped and was followed by a few sniffs. "Yes…I'm fine."

Mya frowned. She didn't sound fine. "Can I come in?" When no confirmation came, Mya pushed aside the curtain and found a red-eyed Sophie sitting on the bench with the straps of her open dress falling off her shoulder.

"Sophie, do you need help?"

She released a dry laugh. "Like you wouldn't believe."

"If you need help with the dress—"

"I don't care about this dress."

Mya stepped into the room, letting the curtain fall behind her. "Then what's wrong? I heard you crying."

Sophie stared up at Mya and her eyes once again filled with tears. "My life's fucked."

To Mya's shock, Sophie suddenly burst into tears. Her sobs shook her slight frame and for a moment, Mya was frozen where she stood. Then, moving instinctively, she sat beside the young girl and began rubbing her back. Sophie leaned into her and cried louder.

Mya didn't know what trauma had brought on this kind of misery, but she offered the girl her silent support. Maybe it would provide her some comfort.

"I'm sure it can't be that bad," Mya offered. "Life always seems hard when—"

"I'm too young to be a single mom," Sophie said through her tears.

Mya's hand stilled. "You're pregnant?"

Sophie nodded, her tears still coming hard. The admission still shocked Mya, but she couldn't understand how the idea of having a baby could bring on this kind of despair. She'd love to have children someday. Guy's baby. Just the thought filled her with an immense joy.

Then she remembered that Sophie *was* young. Maybe three or four years younger than herself. At Sophie's age, she hadn't been ready for marriage, much less raising a baby. She couldn't be sure she was ready now.

That realization struck Mya like nothing else could. Yes, she wanted a family with Guy but not now. They had so much they wanted to accomplish, and they had so much growing they needed to do as a couple before they had children.

But the way they'd been going at it, it might already be too late. Her breath caught in her throat at the thought. She counted the days but couldn't be sure. Her cycle was pretty punctual, but she would have to wait another week or so to be absolutely certain.

"You know, this is not as tragic as you think," Mya said when the girl's emotional storm seemed to pass. "You have your family to support you and—"

Sophie pulled away from her. "No, I don't. My father is ready to marry me off and make me someone else's problem. That's what he called me. A problem!"

Mya frowned. The idea that the mayor would try to arrange a marriage for his young daughter was almost too absurd to be believed. "What about the father? Can't you…"

Sophie scoffed, shaking her head before Mya could finish her sentence. "Forget it. He's not an option.

Serves me right for getting knocked up by a grade-A asshole."

"Well, you shouldn't be forced to get married if you're not ready."

"In case you haven't noticed, my dad's running for mayor and he's not really doing too swell. Ready or not, I have no choice. He says if my pregnancy gets out he's going to for sure lose this election. But it doesn't matter now. In a few more weeks, I won't be able to hide it."

"You can always refuse. He can't drag you to the altar."

"If I don't go through with this, he says he's going to disown me." Sophie leaned her head back against the wall and closed her eyes. "I told you, my life's fucked. I just need to marry the guy he chose and deal."

Mya tensed, remembering what Guy had told her about the mayor pushing his daughter on him. "Who did he tell you to marry?"

Sophie glanced away from her. "Look, I think the sheriff's cute and all, but he is *not* my type. And he's obviously in love with you if he's willing to turn down a promotion and nice raise just to be with you."

Mya stared at her blankly. She didn't know what to say. Though the mayor couldn't have known he'd asked a married man to marry his daughter. But the fact that Guy to keep their marriage intact over his career said how much he really did love her.

"I was so relieved when you came back to town. I thought my dad would drop it, but he thinks the sheriff is the kind of guy that can *handle* me. Whatever. At least now I won't have to try to win his mother over. I was getting a little tired of shopping here. No offense," she added.

Suddenly, Sophie jumped out of her seat. "I should go." She quickly pulled off the new dress. Mya's gaze fell to her abdomen and she noticed the small curve of the woman's lower belly.

She stared at it fixedly.

"Tell Gloria she can keep the dress. Resell it or burn it, I don't care." Sophie threw on her clothes and fled the dressing room.

Mya sat there for a while, still processing everything Sophie had told her. She'd always believed Guy still loved her, but the proof of that made her heart flutter.

She rested her hand over her belly and a terrifying thrill passed through her. The excitement of having Guy's baby made her long to be pregnant. But the thought of being pregnant *now*—when there was still work to be done in their marriage—petrified her.

They weren't ready to be parents—were they?

Guy was greeted by a commotion coming from the kitchen.

The distinct sound of a pot crashing to the ground, followed by a colorful curse, made him smile. He made his way to the kitchen. He couldn't be sure if Mya was preparing a meal or preparing for battle.

"I don't think that pot appreciates you talking about his mother like that," he teased.

She whirled around and he noticed the phone at her ear. She smiled at him as she said into the phone, "Mum, I have to go. Let's talk about this later."

He went into the fridge and grabbed a beer. She continued on with a series of "okays" and "yeses" before she hung up.

"Your mom?"

"Yeah," she muttered, sliding her phone on the counter. "She sends her love."

Guy cocked a brow. "She does?"

Mya chuckled and turned back to the meal she was prepping. "I'm sure she would if she ever got to meet you."

Guy leaned against the counter beside her. He had never gotten the chance to meet Mya's mother, but he could be sure she didn't hold him in high esteem, if her outlook on small-towns and their inhabitants was any indication.

"I heard something about traveling…" he said coolly, tilting the bottle to his lips.

"She just wanted to know when I'll be back to visit."

"And are you going back?" Tension crept into his voice, but he couldn't help it. They were just now trying to make things work between them. Having her leave again—even for a little while—kind of bothered him.

"No, not anytime soon. I'm actually trying to convince her to come here for a visit. I think it'll be the perfect time to tell her and Gloria about us."

"You want to wait that long? It could be a while before she makes it out here for a visit."

He'd thought about telling his mother this week so they could finally make their marriage public, but it looked like that would have to be put on pause.

"I prefer not waiting, but I also don't want to tell my mom over the phone. She already thinks I favor Gloria over her. It'll be easier just to tell them both at the same time."

Guy nodded and took another drink of his beer. He wasn't looking forward to the conversation, and the longer they waited, the harder that conversation was going to get. But he could understand Mya's position in wanting to tell their mothers together. He would wait.

"Don't I get a kiss hello?"

Guy pulled himself out of his thoughts and grinned. Placing his bottle on the counter, he leaned down and kissed her. As usual, what started off as a slow kiss soon turned fiery. He backed her up against the counter and deepened the kiss.

Dinner would have to wait. He needed her now.

He began tugging up her skirt, but she grabbed his wrists and pulled away from him.

"Guy, wait. We have to take a break."

"Why?" he murmured gutturally, trailing his lips down his neck.

She shivered and moved her hands to his shoulders. "I have an appointment at the clinic tomorrow."

He tensed and pulled away from her. "For what?"

Her gaze dropped to his chest. "For birth control. I just think we should, you know, wait...to have kids."

Guy fell silent, unsure how to respond. Waiting made sense. She had just gotten back into his life and their marriage was still a secret to many. Everything about their relationship was new and needed time to grow again.

But he'd always known what he wanted.

He wanted her—and a house full of kids. He was ready to start a family and have what he'd always wanted. And he'd waited long enough.

Mya brought her gaze back up to his. "Waiting is good. Right?"

"Yeah. Right."

"Are you mad?"

He wrapped his arm around her waist and pulled her close. "No. You're right. We should wait." He leaned down and nuzzled her neck. "I'm just bummed this means I can't touch you for a few days."

"Well, we can always do other *thangs*," she said in a mock deep Southerner accent.

"Hmm, what sort of *thangs*?"

Grabbing a large cucumber, she turned back to him and smiled coyly. "Help me with dinner."

Twelve

GUY PUT the last of their dirty dishes into the machine and started it. He wiped down the counters then threw the dish towel over the sink.

It had become routine for them to have breakfast together before they headed off to work. His mouth kicked up when he thought about that morning he'd had *her* for breakfast, then he quickly pushed the thoughts aside. He had firsthand knowledge of how uncomfortable an erection was in this uniform, and he didn't need the discomfort for a second time.

Besides, he was already late for work.

Guy went into the bedroom and grabbed his cell phone and gun belt. The bathroom door was closed but the shower wasn't running. He went to it, a gentle reminder that she was also running late ready on his lips. Yet when he heard her speaking, the words fell away.

"Of course I'm excited I got accepted, but this is a big decision. I just can't uproot my life for another four years."

"Why not?"

Guy recognized her mother's distinct British accent over the phone speaker, and he paused. *Uproot her life?* He didn't mean to eavesdrop, but what the hell was she talking about?

"Zamya, honey, there's nothing for you there. I know you feel you need to be close to your father, but it's time you moved on."

There was a brief pause before Mya spoke again. "Mum, you don't understand. There's a lot more things for me to settle here before I could leave again. There's Daddy's house... There's Guy..."

Her mother made a dismissive sound. "Those are all easy solutions. Find a bank and put the property up for sale. You said it was in horrid condition anyway. As for Guy...I'm sure he'll understand. Going to university would be good for you, honey. And not everyone gets the opportunity to go to Cambridge."

"But I love him, Mum. I don't want to leave him again."

"Well, if he loves you, he wouldn't stop you from trying to improve your life. The sooner you tell him your plans, the better you will feel."

He needed to get out of here.

Guy pushed away from the door, an unexpected tightness settling in his chest, and the pain was suffocating. He slammed out of the house and climbed into his truck, trying to make sense of what he'd just heard.

She was going to leave him? Again?

If her plans had included going back to England, why bother coming back in the first place? Why open the door of possibilities for them when she had no intentions of walking through with him?

The tightness in his chest soon curdled into a mass of anger and resentment that left him sick to his stomach. She'd hurt him before, but it hadn't hurt like this.

Guy cranked the truck and peeled out of the driveway. Everything he'd wanted, everything he'd hoped for, suddenly fizzled away into nothing.

He was a fool.

All that talk about being honest with each other, and yet she'd kept something this big from him. He couldn't understand how she claimed to love him, claim she wanted to make their marriage work, yet have these separate plans in her life going on. Plans that would affect both of them.

Had she even planned on telling him any of this, or did he have another empty bed to look forward to?

The mayor had been wrong. Loving Mya didn't make him weak. It made him stupid. Everything he'd believed about them and their relationship had been painfully true. They weren't compatible with each other. For whatever reason, she couldn't be honest with him—or herself—about what she wanted in her life. But to him, it was painfully clear that she didn't really want a life or future with him.

Not the way he wanted.

We should wait...

Her words last night made it especially clear that settling down and starting a family was not a priority for her, while for him, it was. And he was getting tired of waiting for her to make up her damn mind.

Guy drove past the police station and headed toward the highway. This time he wouldn't wait for her to make the first move. He would finally give her the freedom she obviously wanted and put an end to this mockery of a marriage.

Something was wrong.

Mya didn't know what had caused this complete shutdown in him, but the past week, it was as if Guy had completely pulled away from her. It had been sudden. Actually, it had started the day after they'd talked about her getting on birth control. He had seemed fine with the idea, but now she wondered if it had all been a front.

She didn't think so. He had slept in the same bed with her that night, holding her while they slept. Now, however, he was back to sleeping in the guest room. At first she thought he needed the space, while they waited for her birth control to take effect, but a week later and he was still sleeping in the separate room.

She wanted to confront him about it, but he was making it difficult to do. Most mornings, he was gone before she was awake, and every night he wasn't home until well after she'd gone to bed. There was no mistaking it. He was avoiding her.

But not tonight.

If he wouldn't come to her, she would just go to him and demand that he talk to her. Mya slipped into the empty guest room and crawled into bed. A hint of his male scent surrounded her and she closed her eyes briefly, taking pleasure in feeling close to him again.

Eventually, sleep overcame her. When she woke next, it was to find Guy standing over her, his naked torso visible from the moonlight streaming through the window. Without a word, he slowly drew the sheets back.

Mya sat up and held her breath in anticipation. He pulled her nightshirt over her head then flung it across the room. For a moment, he simply stood there staring down at her body before he peeled off his dark boxers. His swollen erection jutted from his body, and her own body began warming in anticipation of the pleasure awaiting her.

She placed a hand on his shoulders then moved it down to his heated chest. He stiffened, his breath coming out heavy and fast. Before she could react, he pulled her into his arms and kissed her deeply.

Mya leaned into his embrace, deepening the kiss. She gave him everything she had, and he took everything, holding her tightly to him as he devoured her lips with his.

Mya wrapped her arms around his neck and pulled him over her. He followed her down, never breaking contact as he thrust his tongue between her lips. She tasted him, rubbing her tongue along his, and enjoying the feel of him pressed above her as her nipples pushed against his hard chest.

She brought her legs up to cradle him and he settled between her thighs, his hard shaft pushing against her soft, sensitive core. He released a deep groan as he entered her, and she lifted her hips to take more of him. The deliberate thrust was like a delicious caress in the place she needed it most.

Mya tore her lips from his and released a strong gasp. "Guy…"

He trailed his lips down to her neck and sucked strongly at her sensitive skin. Mya shivered, her entire body igniting from the sensation. She laced her fingers through his hair and held him there.

"Please, Guy…I need you."

With a low growl, he thrust deeper into her and they both shuddered from the incredible sensation. Having him nestled so warmly inside her sent shockwaves coursing through her every limb. It had been so long, she almost sobbed from the intense pleasure. He dipped his head low and pulled her nipple into his warm mouth. She arched her back at the intense pleasure as he continued to suck strongly at the sensitive bud.

She rolled her hip up to take more of him as he continued to slowly, gently push into her. She had only a second to savor that moment of tenderness before he began to drive into her with a force that rattled the headboard. It slammed against the wall behind them repeatedly and Mya held on to him tight.

Their love-making had never been this…untamed. He pumped his hips frantically into her, as if he was trying to get as deep inside her as he possibly could. And she was just as wild, clutching his hips and guiding him deeper. With another stroke, he reached her most sensitive spot and she threw her head back and released a loud moan.

The world around her shook as he continued to pump fiercely into her and she could only hold on to him as he took them into unbelievable heights. It wasn't long before she gave in to her mounting desire and came crashing down with enough force to leave her world askew.

In the aftermath of their intense release, she smoothed her palms over his damp shoulders, enjoying the feel of him in that small touch.

"I love you, Guy."

He didn't repeat the words, but she hadn't expected him to. She was content to have him with her again.

For the rest of the night, they made love again and again, until she couldn't remember what it felt like to be without him.

He was insatiable.

Minutes passed with them locked in each other's arms, and she wanted them to stay like that forever. But she sensed the shift in him, felt the withdrawal, and knew what was coming.

He began to pull away from her, and Mya tightened her arms around his neck.

"Please, Guy," she whispered into his ear. "Don't leave."

He tensed above her then fell back into her arms. He shifted until they lay on their sides and he gathered her in his arms. With a small sigh of contentment, Mya wrapped her arms around him again and held him tight…

But it wasn't until later that night, when the cool air of the drafty room woke her from a deep sleep, that she found herself alone in the wide bed. Fighting back her sobs, she curled into her side and tried to make sense of tonight.

The smell of coffee woke her.

Mya jumped out of bed and pulled on her discarded nightshirt. She couldn't let him leave this morning without talking to him about last night first.

She found him sitting at the kitchen, finishing his coffee. He glanced up at her when she walked in, his expression blank and unreadable. He had his work uniform on but didn't seem to be in any rush. Had he been waiting for her to get up?

"Guy, we need to talk."

He got up from his seat and placed his mug in the sink. "I know."

A long silence fell between them and Mya blew out a frustrated breath.

"So start talking. Tell me what's wrong. Why are you avoiding me?"

He turned to her, his gaze cold and direct. "I think it's time we ended this. The papers are on the table. Just sign it and we can get this over with."

Mya turned to the table and saw the neatly stacked pile of legal documents. Her heart sank.

He wants a divorce?

She knew what they were and didn't bother asking for confirmation. What she couldn't understand was why. Things had been going so well—before this week from hell, anyway. Was that why he'd been avoiding her this week? Had he always planned to serve her these and just didn't know how to approach her?

But last night... She remembered their love-making, remembered how deep he had come into her, how he couldn't seem to get enough of her. Her body quivered from the vivid memory.

Mya turned back to him, but she concentrated her gaze on his chest. "I don't understand… Last night…you…we… I thought things were going to be different. Maybe get better again."

"Why? Because we had sex?"

Her gaze flew up to his and her back stiffened at the crudeness of his tone. "Was that all it was for you? Sex?"

He frowned. "What were you expecting, Mya? I was horny and you were avail—"

"Shut up."

The vehemence in her voice surprised even her. Her hands were balled into fists at her sides and fought to control the nausea that churned in her stomach. He was trying to make nothing out of last night with his cruel words, but she was certain he hadn't been immune to the intensity of their union.

"I get that you might still be pissed with me, but don't reduce what we shared last night to just meaningless sex. It was more than that, and we both know it."

He cursed and ran his hand through his hair. She recognized the uncertain gesture and her anger slowly dissipated.

"You talk about being honest, so be honest with yourself, Mya. You don't really want to be married."

"Maybe that was true two years ago," she admitted, shifting uncomfortably, "but that's not the case now."

"Then what about Cambridge? You didn't tell me about that."

She stared at him, stunned. "How'd you know?"

"Does it matter? I know you got accepted and that you plan on leaving." He scoffed. "So much for being honest with each other."

She shut her eyes briefly. "It's not like that. I never planned to go. I just...I haven't found the right time to tell my mom that I'm not moving back."

He fell silent for a moment. "Or do you mean you couldn't find the right words to tell me you were leaving again?"

"You know that's not true. I love you, Guy, and I know you still love me." For a moment, the hardness left his expression. The hurt vulnerability in his green eyes tugged at her heart. With hesitant steps, she took the few short steps toward him and gingerly placed her palm on his chest. "Stop fighting it. Stop fighting *me*. Give us a chance. We owe each other that."

In an instant, he went rigid. "We don't owe each other anything, Mya. Don't mistake a great night of screwing for anything more. We both had needs and we did something about it. We may be great together in bed, but that's it. There's nothing else besides that for us."

Mya shook her head, denying his hurtful words. "You don't mean that."

Something dangerous flashed in his eyes. "I don't?"

Before she could react, he grabbed her by the waist, lifted her high and dropped her down on the counter. He ripped open his slacks and pushed up her nightshirt. Mya stared in shocked amazement at the swiftness of his movements.

Without much preparation, he moved between her legs and drove into her with unbelievable strength. Mya cried out by the jolting entry, clinging to him as he pounded into her. Last night proved just how much she loved the way he lost control and gave all of himself to her. But this felt different. It was as if he wasn't truly with her.

Wanting to find their connection again, Mya tried to kiss him, but his face remained buried in the crook of her neck. Suddenly, he went rigid. Once he found his release, he pulled away from her and began adjusting himself.

Her body quivered as she slid down the counter, unsure of how she felt in that moment. *Used* was a pretty apt word. She leaned against the counter, waiting for her legs to stop their trembling while she tried to make sense of what just happened.

"Why did you do that?"

He shrugged. "See how I can fuck and forget you, too?"

Mya went cold. Those weren't just hurtful words of a heartbroken man. He wanted to take away any shred of dignity she had, any last ounce of self-respect.

He wanted to break her.

"You bastard." Without thinking, she struck him in the jaw with all she had. His head whipped around, but he remained eerily still. "I'm not your sex toy or some *thing* you can treat this way! I'm your wife, damn it, and—"

Suddenly, he erupted and her words were cut off in an instant. He grabbed her by the waist and shoved her against the counter, his hands still around her.

"You've *never* been my wife!" His face was twisted in a rage, and only inches from her. "You lost the right to call yourself that the moment you walked out on me. On *us*."

His eyes were like lasers as they searched hers. She didn't know what he saw in them, or what he was looking for, but suddenly he released her as if she were made of spikes.

"But then there had never been an *us*, had there? You're too damn self-centered."

Her gaze moved over his. "Why are you trying to hurt me?"

"Because you broke my fucking heart."

Tears suddenly welled in her eyes and she couldn't stop them as they began to course down her cheeks. "I didn't mean to."

He let out a harsh sound and before she knew it, he had her in his arms.

"Damn it, stop crying," he said gruffly, his hand gently rubbing the back of her neck. "As much as I wanted you, I should have known we didn't stand a chance. We didn't then and we don't now."

Mya released a shuddering breath. "Guy, please don't say that. I love—"

He pulled away from her. "Stop. I can't keep doing this with you, so just stop."

She took a step toward him, refusing to believe he was ready for them to end. But again, he pulled away from her.

"You walked out on me before, Mya. Can you possibly understand what that did to me? You made me feel unwanted, and I never thought I would feel that with you. And I'm not going to let you do that to me again."

Tears once again blurred her vision. His pain was hers and she realized that there was nothing she could do or say to ease it for him. That was probably the most painful part of it all.

Without another word, he turned to leave but paused. For a moment, she held out hope that he would come back to her.

"I think it's time you found someplace else to stay."

With those final words, he slammed out of the house.

Thirteen

A HEAVY PIT settled in his stomach as Guy returned to an empty house.

There was no Jeep Wrangler in his driveway and he didn't need to go far to know she was gone. The house was eerily silent, and the energy that had once been tangible in the simple space was gone. Guy went into the kitchen where they'd had their fight that morning.

He leaned against the counter, thinking of how fast he'd taken her. He didn't know what had come over him. He'd let his anger and need drive his actions—the same burning, incessant hunger he felt for her all these years. No matter how many times he took her, he would never get enough of her.

He also remembered the harsh words he'd said to her and the crushed looked she'd given him…

The memory of her haunted expression ate at him. Hurting her with his callous words hadn't made him feel vindicated, and telling her to leave his home only left him feeling as empty and hollow as his home.

Guy couldn't make sense of what he was feeling. He thought getting Mya out of his life for good would stop the constant ache he felt for her. But it didn't.

He still wanted her—still ached for her.

"Damn it."

He ran his hand over his face. By now, he'd half expected his mother to call him, demanding to know why he had sent Mya away. He figured Mya would have gotten settled into his mother's house by now. He found it odd that she hadn't called him, incensed on Mya's behalf.

Guy cursed again. No matter how he felt about Mya right now, he couldn't rest tonight not knowing where she was. With another curse, he pulled out his cell and called his mother.

"Well, this is a nice surprise," his mother said crisply. "You calling me for a change?"

Guy ignored her sarcasm. "Ma, did Mya get to your place yet?"

There was a short pause. "No. Was she supposed to come by tonight?"

"No… I—we had a fight and I thought she would head over to your place."

The pause was longer this time. "What makes you think she would come to me?"

Guy scoffed. "She always goes to you. When she's done running from her problems, anyway."

"Why would she be running? What did you do to her this time?"

What I should have done from the beginning, he thought harshly. Guy glanced at the table and saw the divorce papers still neatly stacked there. He went to the table and picked up the sheaf of papers. He flipped through to the back, and in bold black ink was her signature.

He stared at it for a while, not quite understanding that hollowness that seemed to grow and expand in him. He'd wanted this divorce, so why did it hurt so damn bad?

Guy bit back a curse, slamming the papers on the table.

"Guy Gregory Lawson, answer me."

He blew out a heavy breath. "I told her to leave, Ma."

Even to his ears, the words made him sound like the biggest bastard. But her leaving was for the best. He couldn't keep his hands off her, and building false illusions around them being a real couple wasn't helping either one of them. The harsh reality was that they would never be like they once were.

Yet another part of him missed her already. He missed her presence and just having her near, under his roof.

"You jackass." His mother's harsh insult jarred him back to their conversation. "I can't believe you kicked her out. When you knew she had no place else to go."

"She has you."

"And you really think she's going to feel comfortable coming to me after you humiliated her like this? Are you really that dense about women? About *her*?"

Guy rubbed the back of his neck, feeling the sting of his mother's words. In retrospect, he probably should have given her some time to find a place. But he always assumed she would go to his mother. They were close, and he couldn't think of anyone else around town she would feel comfortable reaching out to.

"Did she say anything to you today at the shop? Where she was going?"

"She didn't come in. She said she wasn't feeling well. No thanks to you, I'm sure."

Guy ground his teeth. "Would you just let me know when she gets to your place?"

"You better hope she does. And when she gets here, you better have your apology waiting, you big…*jackass!*"

Guy's head jerked from the abrupt disconnection. He stared at the phone. He hoped his mother would get past her anger long enough to call him as soon as Mya got to her place.

But when three hours passed and no word came from his mother, Guy began to really worry. His mother could be punishing him by keeping him waiting, but something in his gut told him that wasn't the case. Quelling his rising anxiety, Guy dialed his mother again.

"Ma, just tell me she's with you," Guy said abruptly, not in the mood for another of her snide comments.

Something in his voice must have alerted her of his anxiety, because traces of her earlier anger were gone. In its place was a quiet concern.

"She's not here, Guy. I've been waiting at home all evening. Where do you think she could have gone? It's getting late."

"Do you think she went to the shop?"

"No, she wouldn't be there. There's no place for her to sleep there."

"Then she must have gone to a motel."

"I don't think so."

His mother was right. In their town, the closest motel to Cedar Bend was an hour's drive away. There were a few bed & breakfasts that catered to the occasional tourist or visitor and he highly doubted she would go asking for a room. Guy cursed.

"Listen, I'll give her a call," his mother offered. "Find out where she is and then I'll call you back."

Guy preferred to call her himself and demand to know where she was, but he knew she would most likely disregard his call. But when his mother called to tell him that Mya's phone had taken her straight to voicemail, he wasted no more time. He jumped into his truck and drove through town. There weren't many places for her to hide. And she had only ever known three homes— his, his mother's, and...

Damn it.

Guy slammed on the breaks. Her father's home. That's where she was. He knew that with every fiber in his being, and the thought made the hairs on the back of his neck rise. The house was uninhabitable, and yet he knew she would ignore all the signs and settle herself in there.

Unless that was her plan—to have him come get her. She knew he wouldn't let her stay there, but then again, maybe he should teach her a lesson and have her spend the night there.

The thought of her in that big drafty home, however, with the weak floors and foundation, made him balk at the idea. He couldn't leave her in there and she knew it.

She knew him too well.

With a vicious curse, Guy whipped the truck around and sped down the road toward her father's old home.

Mya coughed as she shook out the dusty coverlet over her old bed.

Perhaps coming back to her old home had not been a wise decision, but then again, she hadn't been thinking clearly. The shock of Guy's words had eventually worn off, but the pain in her heart was still there and heavier than ever.

He doesn't love me anymore.

That harsh realization made her stomach clench painfully. Guy was right. It was too late for them. She was all out of options and ideas to convince him that she loved him and that she wanted to make their relationship work. She couldn't force him to accept something he didn't want, and he clearly didn't want her.

Not anymore.

Mya sat down on the edge of the bed, her thin nightshirt offering very little heat against the chill in the air. Or maybe it was the chill inside her that hadn't gone away after their fight that morning.

Either way, it wouldn't change anything. She would have to spend the night in the drafty house until she could get power and heat connected tomorrow.

Mya crawled onto the thin mattress and lay there listening to the soft creaks of the old house and the whispers of the night creatures.

She still couldn't believe how much she had overestimated Guy's feelings for her. She should have seen how cold and withered his heart was toward her— much like her father's home. She was a fool for thinking she could fix something that never stood a real chance. She'd tried to take something they'd once shared and build a future with it, but she'd been naïve. They had clearly grown too far apart.

Eventually, she shut her eyes, but sleep—like Guy and the love he once held for her—was far from reach…

A loud crash jerked her awake.

Mya didn't know how long she'd been asleep, but the sudden noise downstairs jolted her out of her shallow slumber. She hadn't been asleep long. It was still dark outside and the moon was still high and shining through the bare windows.

There was another loud thud downstairs, and Mya jumped out of bed. She grabbed the flashlight she'd brought up with her and held it tight in her hand. She wasn't sure what she would encounter downstairs, but her main concern was getting out of the house. The last thing she wanted was to be trapped upstairs with a roaming animal—or lunatic.

She was partway downstairs when she realized she'd left her phone and car keys in the bedroom.

Damn it.

Mya took another step down the squeaky steps and winced with every groan and creak it made. She reached the bottom of the landing only to be met with a large chest and a grip as hard as iron.

She screamed and swung the flashlight wildly. It connected with something just as hard.

"*Shit.*"

"Guy?"

"Who else?"

In the darkness, she could see him rubbing his shoulder. "What are you doing creeping around down here?"

"I was looking for you. I tried calling, but it must be dead."

She hadn't even realized. Guess her cell wouldn't have been much use for her anyway. "The power's not on."

"Obviously. Now where's your things? I'm taking you home."

Mya frowned. "I am home."

Guy scoffed, glancing around the old place. "Calling this place a home is a stretch, don't you think?"

Her back stiffened. "It's more a home than yours will ever be."

Tense silence fell between them. She was getting tired of the arguing and the insults. She didn't want to hurt him—she had never wanted that. But she wasn't going to allow him to break her spirit either.

"Guy, I can't stop you from hating me. Nothing I've tried has worked and I'm tired of running against your wall. I love you, but I'm not going to continue being your speed bag while you decide whether you still want me or not."

"I don't hate you."

But you don't love me either.

"Well, that's a relief. Now please leave."

"Damn it, Mya. This house is dangerous. There's a lot of work to be done and you can't stay here."

"Well, it's all I have left, so I'm staying."

"I'm not leaving you here. It's not safe. I will drag you out of here, if I have to."

"If you think I'm going to set a foot back inside your house—"

"I'll take you to my mother's," he said through gritted teeth. "But I'm not leaving you here."

"Guy—"

"Where's your things?" he interrupted again. "We're leaving here. *Now.*"

Mya was quickly losing the reins on her patience. "I'm not going anywhere with you!"

He cursed then bounded up the stairs two at a time. "Just wait there."

"No." She ran after him. "*Get out.* I said I'm not—"

Suddenly, a loud crack thundered around them. They both froze.

"What was that?" Mya wasn't sure why she whispered the question, but something in her felt that any slight noise or movement would have the house caving all around them.

Guy was several steps above, and he carefully turned back to face her. "We're going to have to come back for your things later. I don't think these stairs are going to hold our weight."

There was another sharp crack as Guy took another step down. This time, the wood shuddered beneath their feet. Mya sucked in a breath and grabbed for the stair rails.

"Guy, be careful!"

"I will. Just slowly head back down. Hold the rails."

That wasn't a problem. Her grip around it was unshakeable. It was getting her legs to move that was the problem.

"Mya, get down the stairs."

She shook her head, staring at his feet. He was much higher on the stairs than she was, and she was afraid any movements she made would weaken the already fragile structure.

"Not until you can come down with me."

"I'll be right behind you." He took another step down. "We need to even out the weight, so I need you to get down."

He was right, of course. But she wished he wasn't already so high up. She took a step back and he followed suit. She didn't know if it was all in her head, but the wood beneath her felt unbelievably frail. She didn't know why she hadn't realized that before.

"That's good. Nice and easy."

She took another step back, but miscalculated her step and nearly went flying back. With a loud shriek, she instinctively reached out in front of her.

"Mya!"

Guy rushed down the steps to grab hold of her, but he wasn't close enough.

Suddenly, something resembling an explosion resounded in the old house and the floors caved beneath them. Mya had only a split second to register what had happened before Guy's horrified face disappeared from her sight.

Fourteen

THERE WAS NOISE EVERYWHERE.

Hurried voices, loud beeping, the grating of metal against concrete. Yet despite the acute noise flooding Guy's senses, nothing compared to the pain shooting along his left side.

The pain in his shoulder was like a jolt to his system. Guy peeled his eyes open and was met by a blinding white light. He winced and turned his head away.

"Sheriff? Stay with us. We're almost there."

Guy gritted his teeth. *Almost where?*

The last thing he remembered was going home.

It had been empty. It shouldn't have been... Mya should have been there... But she'd left him.

No.

He'd told her to leave. But he'd gone to get her back. He didn't want her to go... He had to get her back. He had to save her... But he hadn't gotten to her in time. Her horrified face flashed in his eyes before it had disappeared.

Mya.

"Sheriff, please calm down."

He hadn't realized he'd shouted the word until that moment. He struggled to sit up but felt two hands holding him firmly down. Intense pain shot down his arm as he struggled to come up, but he ignored it.

"My wife! Where is she?"

"Damn it, Alex. Hold him."

"Mya!"

"Sheriff, you have to calm down. Your wife is fine. She's being treated for minor cuts, but we have to get you prepared for surgery."

Guy couldn't make out the woman's face, the light was still so damn bright, but knowing that Mya was okay eased some of his panic.

"I want to see her." He tried to sit up again, but this time it was the growing pain on his left shoulder that kept him down. He turned his head, and that was when he saw it—the long piece of wood protruding from his shoulder. One look at it sent another shock wave of pain.

"Fuck."

"Relax, sheriff. We just gave you something for the pain. Once it kicks in, we will have…"

The doctor's words faded as the world around him began to blur. He suddenly felt numb all over and was thankful for it. He was tired of hurting, tired of the relentless pain of being angry and feeling rejected.

He was so damn tired.

But she was safe, and that was all that mattered to him. He let his mind succumb to the void until he felt nothing.

Mya paced outside the operating room doors, twisting and untwisting the pale blue hospital gown she'd been given. The hospital staff had let her be when they realized they would have to forcibly remove her from that spot.

Her stomach was twisted in knots, and her mind raced with the horrifying possibilities that he wouldn't be okay. Just thinking of how long it had taken her to operate his police radio to call for help, how they had dug him out of the pile of broken wood. Just thinking about the way one long, jagged piece had protruded gruesomely from his body made her ill. And the blood...

Mya shook her head. He was going to be okay. He had to be. The alternative was too unbearable to consider.

"Mya? Oh, thank God."

She turned to find Gloria rushing to her. She pulled her into a tight hug and Mya clung to her.

"Where is he? Where is Guy?"

"He's still in surgery. I think. They won't tell me anything." Her voice thickened with tears, and Gloria pulled her into another tight hug.

"What happened out there?"

Mya took a steadying breath and filled Gloria in on her stupidity. She'd known the house was unsafe and yet she had gone there anyway, putting herself and Guy in danger.

"I did this," Mya whispered. "I shouldn't have gone there. He tried to tell me but I wouldn't listen, and now—"

The tears started again, clouding her vision and Mya covering her face. She didn't want Gloria to see her fall apart, but she couldn't stop the tears that fell. Being at the hospital again brought back all of the same horrible memories, the same fears and panic. She couldn't lose Guy too. She couldn't. The unfairness of it all weighed on her and she broke down.

Gloria grabbed her arm and shook her. "Mya, stop this. You can't fall apart on me now. I can't do this without you."

Mya nodded and took a shuddering breath. The last thing Gloria needed was to think the worst about her only child. She wiped her eyes and noticed the pallor on Gloria's face. Behind her glasses, her eyes were red and glassy.

Shame over her weakness filled Mya. If Gloria could manage to hold it together, she needed to at least try.

Mya took another calming breath. "You're right, Gloria. I'm sorry."

Suddenly the door to the operating room opened and the doctor she had spoken to earlier came out.

"Mrs. Lawson?"

"Yes."

She and Gloria spoke in unison, and Gloria glanced at her in surprise. Mya slid her gaze from hers and asked the doctor anxiously, "How is he?"

"He's stable right now. We removed the wood and splinters found in the wound, but he lost a lot of blood. We will need your permission to do an immediate blood transfusion."

"Yes."

"No."

Mya glanced at Gloria in surprise.

"I don't want him getting some stranger's blood," Gloria snapped. "Do you know how dangerous that is? What if he got infected with something? I've heard cases of people dying from those things. So *no*."

"But Gloria, this could save his life," Mya said, incredulous. She turned to the doctor. "I want you to do everything you can for him."

Gloria inhaled sharply. "How dare you, Mya. I'm his mother and——"

"I'm his *wife*."

Gloria's eyes rounded with shock and disbelief flooded her gaze. Suddenly, Mya was tired of all the lies and secrets.

"We've been married for two years now. We got married at the county court."

Astonishment filled Gloria's expression. Then, to Mya's disappointment, her face reddened and the outrage in her eyes was unmistakable.

Mya turned away from her icy glare and said to the doctor, "Please do whatever you need to save him."

Guy woke to find both Mya and his mother peering down at him. It took a moment for him to orient himself, but the memories—and bright lights—came crashing through him and he shut his eyes again from the onslaught.

"Guy?" Mya slipped her hand into his and a sense of calm washed through him. "How do you feel?"

He cracked his eyes open again. "Like a million bucks."

That garnered a few weak smiles from both of them.

"You look like a million bucks." His mother patted his scruffy cheeks. "Welcome back, sleeping beauty."

His lips curved in a wry smile.

"How long have I been here?"

"Two days. You've been in and out of it. Don't you remember?" Mya asked.

"Some," he said. He tried to shift but found it difficult. "It's mostly a blur. What happened?"

"The stairs collapsed and you fell through," Mya explained. "Your shoulder was impacted and they had to do emergency surgery. And a blood transfusion."

"But don't worry honey. Luckily, I was an exact match, so you still have your mama's blood flowing in you."

"Do you need anything?" Mya asked. "Can I get you anything?"

"I'm fine." Actually, he was sore all over, but he hated to see the anxiety in her eyes.

"Are you sure?"

He squeezed her hand in reassurance. "Yes, love. I'm fine."

"Mya, would you excuse us for a moment? I'd like to talk to my son. Alone."

At his mother's terse request, Mya's lips tightened. The tension between them was palpable. Mya looked like she wanted to refuse but thought better of it. Instead, she leaned down and placed a light kiss on his lips.

"I'll be right outside if you need me," she murmured.

Guy waited until she left before he turned to his mother. "What's going on with you two?"

His mother's gentle rubbing on his arm was still light, but her gaze was sharp. "Don't take that tone with me, Guy Lawson. Not when I'm this angry with you."

Guy's brows pulled together. "What did I do now?"

"Mind explaining to me why the hell you and Mya got married at the courthouse? And two years, Guy? You kept this from me for two years!"

He sighed. "She told you."

"Yes!" she snapped. "But what I don't understand is why you wanted to keep this a secret from me. I love you and Mya. I wanted to be there, damn it."

"Ma, don't cry. We were going to tell you, but…things just weren't going to work out."

"What do you mean? Why'd you two rush to the altar in the first place if you weren't going to give it a chance?" Suddenly, she gasped and her hand flew to her throat. "Was she pregnant?"

"No, it wasn't like that. I married her because I love her, and I thought she loved me too."

His mother frowned and cocked her head to the side. "Of course she loves you. You should have seen the way she took charge to make sure you got the best treatment. I wasn't sure whether I should be pleased, or incensed, that she was basically taking over my job."

Guy was a bit surprised by what his mother was telling him. He'd half expected Mya to break down or shut down, much like she had when her father had been rushed to the hospital with his critical injuries. He'd always believed Mya would run instead of face the tough moments in life, like she had in the past. But if what his mother was saying was true, then he really had underestimated the woman Mya was now.

"What I don't understand," his mother continued, "is if you two got married two years ago, that means you got married right before she left for England?"

"Yeah," Guy said stiffly, not liking where his mother was going with this.

She was silent for a long while. Then she asked, "Before or after?"

Guy sighed. He knew exactly what she was asking. "After the funeral. Then she left me after we— On our wedding night."

He couldn't mask the bitterness in his tone and he didn't bother trying. Everything was all out in the open, and whether his mother agreed with him or not, whether she approved of their situation, didn't change the fact that they are in a marriage that would soon come to an end.

"Why?" she finally asked. "Why the rush? The secrecy?"

"I just wanted to take care of her. I loved her. If she hadn't run off, there would have been no reason to keep it from you."

His mother sighed and continued rubbing his arm. "Oh, honey. Your heart was in the right place, but what you did was stupid. She had just lost her father. What made you think she was ready for marriage? Because you were?"

Guy frowned, taking exception to his mother's accusations. "She could have told me she wasn't ready. Instead of going through with it then walking out before we had a chance to start anything."

"And what did she say when you asked her?"

Guy tightened his lips and looked away from her. He hadn't actually asked Mya, but getting married was something they'd talked about before. He'd wanted to wait until the time was right, until he had the chance to talk to Marvin and ask for her hand. But then Marvin was fatally wounded on the job, and Guy had been eager to make her his—before God forbid he would lose the opportunity.

"You didn't ask her, did you? That's what I thought. Now I can see why she ran off to England."

"I'm glad one of us does," he muttered.

"And if you took a minute to put yourself in her shoes, you would too. She had just lost her father and you thought the smart move was to take off and get married? Someplace where she had none of her friends or family around? That was a really selfish move, Guy."

Guy thought about his mother's words and thought back on that day he'd driven to the county courthouse, with Mya sitting silently beside him. She'd been withdrawn that night, and he had chalked it up to the stress she had been under lately.

"I thought she needed me," he muttered.

"She did, Guy. But she also needed to grieve her father. How was she supposed to do that and be your new wife? Do you honestly think that's how she wanted to start a new life with you? In mourning? You backed her into a corner, so naturally she panicked."

Guy stared up at the ceiling and accepted what a mess he'd made of things. For him, getting married had seemed like the best way for him to show her how much he loved and wanted her. He'd just wanted to make her happy again. To make them both happy.

Instead, he'd managed to do the opposite. Maybe if he'd given her time and space, he could have saved himself two years of heartache and resentment.

"You were right, Ma. I'm an idiot."

"Like I said, honey. Your heart was in the right place, but a girl like Mya deserves to have a proper wedding day, with your friends and family around to celebrate with you both."

Again, his mother was right. He needed to fix this. He thought about the divorce papers—the papers she had signed—and thought about the many ways he could destroy them.

He wasn't going to let her go that easy. She was his. And if his near death experienced had taught him anything, it was that he wasn't ready to live without her.

Fifteen

"I CAN'T BELIEVE I'm an accomplice to this. Aunt Gloria and Mya are going to have my head for this."

"You'll be fine," Guy said, pulling on his shirt carefully.

Mike snorted. "Not when they find out I'm breaking you out of here."

"It's called checking myself out," Guy muttered. "I've had enough of this bed and the food."

"Well, if anyone asks, I'm going to say you made me do it."

"Sure, whatever. Just get me out of here."

After five long days, Guy was ready to get back to his normal life. And though he was scheduled to be released tomorrow, Guy hadn't wanted to wait that long. Not that he didn't appreciate the coddling, but between his mother and Mya, he felt as if he was suffocating from their constant hovering.

Today had been the first time he'd gotten them to leave the hospital and look after themselves and the shop. Though what he really wanted was to get Mya alone so they could talk. But his mother refused to leave his bedside, which was just as well. The kind of conversation they needed to have shouldn't be done while he was flat on his back.

Luckily, Mike had agreed to come get him, albeit reluctantly.

In his cousin's car, Guy maneuvered himself so that he didn't aggravate his sore shoulder. His arm was in a sling and he was pumped with pain relievers, yet he still felt an occasional twinge of pain.

But that wouldn't stop him from carrying out his plan.

"I need you to make a few stops."

Mike glanced at him suspiciously. "Where to? Because I would much rather take you home and let your *wife* deal with you."

Guy's lips curved up. "Is that really how you're going to treat your injured cousin?"

"Yes. You got too used to ruling from the throne that was your hospital bed. It'll be nice to have you back to reality."

Guy chuckled, though he was just as glad to be back to his life, too. He remembered the promise he'd made to Mya in his head the night she'd been at his side. He had been in a state of unconscious reality, probably from the medicine, but he remembered Mya's words clearly that night as she'd held his hand...

"Daddy once told me about the time you were called in for a shoplifter stealing groceries. Instead of arresting the man, he said you paid for the stuff. I don't know if Daddy told you, but he was so proud of you. You are the kind of police officer we need more of, he said. And I knew then that I was madly in love with you. So I need you to get better, Guy, because we still need you."

And it had been those words that had seen him through his fog of pain and lethargy.

"Is everything all set for next week?"

Mike nodded. "Yep. The contractors looked through the damage and noted all the weak points around the house. Obviously, the stairs are going to be the bulk of the work, but the good news is that the foundation is still solid, so that will cut some time on the repairs."

Guy nodded, relieved that the house wasn't a complete loss. Repairing Mya's father's house was an idea he had thought long and hard about. He knew the home had been in her father's family for a long time. He didn't know if she would plan to keep it or sell it. He would leave that decision to her. But his hope was that they could restart their lives together in the renovated home—and restore the happy memories and sense of security she had lost.

To do that, he had to do one more thing...

"Actually, I need to make two more stops then you're off the hook."

Mike sighed. "What do you need now?"

Guy grinned. "I need to buy a ring."

"So when are you going to tell your mother?"

Mya shrugged. "Maybe tonight."

She knew she was putting off the much-needed conversation, but after Gloria's reaction, she wasn't looking forward to it more than ever. She and Gloria had just gotten back to the way things had been between them before she'd found out about their secret marriage. It wasn't the way Mya would have liked Gloria to find out, but it was finally out in the open and she needed to do the same with her mother.

She'd learned the hard way that secrets helped no one.

"Well, I'm sure she won't be happy with how you two handled things, but at least she'll be getting an awesome son-in-law. And the sooner she knows, the better."

Mya agreed, except she didn't know how soon after she would be announcing their impending divorce. She and Guy hadn't had a chance to talk about the signed divorce papers in his dresser drawer. She had placed them there when she'd stopped by his home to pick up a change of clothes for his release tomorrow.

As much as she didn't want to dissolve their marriage, she didn't want him to feel forced to carry out a promise—or commitment—he no longer wanted. She would help see him through his recovery, and then after... She could only hope he found real happiness with someone else.

Tears filled her eyes at the depressing thought, but she quickly blinked them away.

The bell chimed on the door, signaling an arriving customer. Mya turned with a greeting on her lips, but it immediately fell away when she saw Guy walking toward her with Mike following right behind.

"Guy!" Gloria exclaimed. "What are you doing out of the hospital?"

Mike pointed at Guy. "He made me do it."

While Gloria lit into her nephew, Mya kept her gaze on Guy. He looked better, healthier than he had before, though he was still a bit pale for her liking. But to see him walking around again, despite the sling around his arm, filled her with such relief. He really was going to be all right.

He stopped in front of her and said in a low voice, "Can we go for a walk?"

"I have two hours left on my shift," she murmured. "I would have to ask Gloria."

He shook his head, came around the counter, and pulled her to his side. "Ma, I'm taking Mya out for a walk. We'll be right back."

"A walk?" Gloria sputtered. "You're barely out of the hospital and you want to exert yourself. Mya, talk to him!"

Mya looked up at him and saw the mysterious gleam in his green eyes. She couldn't help but smile. "You look good."

He grinned. "I feel good. Now come on."

Ignoring his mother's grumbling, he led Mya outside into the crisp spring air. She forgot how fast March had arrived, but was grateful for it. Soon the flowers would bloom along Main Street and their small town would come alive with the signs of new beginnings.

"Where are you taking me?"

He hesitated then said, "Promise Lane."

She frowned. "Why?"

"So I can do things over. Do them right."

"What are you talking about?"

He said nothing as they walked down the cobbled path to the arched bridge of Promise Lane. Soon the path would be brightened with colorful flowers and rich green leaves. For now, the branches were bare with the lingering signs of winter.

They came to a stop in the middle of the path and Mya stared up at him. He appeared a bit nervous, and unconsciously, Mya squeezed his hand.

"Guy, what is it?"

He cleared his throat and began, "Three years ago, on this spot, I promised to love and protect you. Always. I meant every word of it then and I do now. But I haven't done a very good job of that."

Mya bit her lip, trying to control the slight trembling in them. "You fell through a flight of stairs for me, Guy. I think you're doing a fine job."

The corner of his lips curved up. "If it wasn't for me, we wouldn't have been in that position in the first place. I shouldn't have pushed you away like that. I love you, Mya. And I need you in my life."

She stared at him searchingly, her heart filling with love. "I need you in my life too, Guy. When I left here, it had nothing to do with you or us. I always wanted to be your wife. I just need to find *me* first so that I could be that for you."

"I know, babe. And if I could do that day all over again, I would have waited to do it the right way."

"What do you mean?"

He reached out and trailed his finger along her jaw. "You deserve the best, and I promise I'll do everything in my power to give that to you."

"Oh, Guy, all I've ever wanted was *you*. That's all."

He grinned then reached into his pocket and pulled out a small black box. She frowned in confusion before realization hit her and she sucked in a sharp breath.

Suddenly, he struggled down to one knee, and she tugged at his good arm.

"What are you doing? Get up before you fall!"

He chuckled. "Too late. I've already fallen for you, babe. Hard. Now, let me do this the right way."

"But Guy...we're already married," she said in a fierce whisper.

He gave her a lopsided grin. "And I want the whole world to know it."

Mya covered her cheeks with her hands, surprised by the small crowd that had suddenly gathered. She was embarrassed and delighted all at once.

Snapping the small ring box open, he held it out to her, but Mya barely noticed it through happy tears that blurred her vision.

"Zamya Daniels, will you do me the honor of officially taking my last name?"

A bubble of laughter burst from her and she threw her arms around his neck, careful not to jolt his injured shoulder.

"Yes. If you insist."

He looped his good arm around her and pulled her close. "Yes, baby, I insist."

His lips fitted neatly against hers, as if they had found their home, and she released a soft sigh filled with an indescribable bliss.

Epilogue

Six weeks later…

"MYA, honey, you can't be late to your own wedding."

She glanced at Gloria but was immediately reprimanded.

"Zamya, hold still, else you'll end up with raccoon eyes."

"Sorry, Mum," she muttered. "And Gloria, stop worrying. We have time. After all, they can't get started without the bride."

"That's right," her mother agreed and Gloria just harrumphed.

Mya held back a smile, not wanting to mess with the work her mother was creating on her face. She was thrilled, not only because today was her wedding day, but because she had the two women she cared most about at her side. Her mother had made the transatlantic flight alone just to be at their small backyard wedding.

With the money Guy was investing in the repairs to her father's house, their wedding had turned out to be a modest affair, but she didn't care. She was about to profess her love and commitment to the man of her dreams, in front of her friends and family, and that was all that mattered to her.

"Okay, all done, sweetie. Take a look."

Mya held the mirror to her face and gaped at the woman staring back at her. Thanks to her mother, she was breathtaking.

She jumped off of the stool and gave her mother a tight hug.

"Thanks, Mum!"

"You're welcome, darling. Now let's get you into that dress."

Gloria pulled down the simple vintage gown from the hanger and brought it to her. Mya's heart skipped at the sight of it.

The ivory-colored wedding dress was her mother's, worn during her second marriage. It was exceptionally beautiful with its vintage embroidered lace along the solid cap-sleeved bodice. A few floral lace patterns accented the airy A-line tulle skirt, but was subtle enough to leave the dress exquisitely simple.

Mya's sentimentality got the better of her, and she began to tear up. It wasn't just from the opportunity to start a new tradition in her family by someday passing the dress down to her own daughter. For her, the old vintage dress symbolized the true second chance that she and Guy would have.

"No, no, no." Her mother grabbed a tissue. "Save the tears for *after* the 'I do's.'"

Mya dabbed around her eyes, trying not to laugh.

"Claire's right," Gloria said. "Today is a joyous day for all of us." She cupped her face. "I finally get to have you as a daughter."

Tears brimmed her eyes again but she blinked them away. On a day like this, when she was missing her daddy fiercely, she just needed to take a moment to appreciate what she was gaining.

A new family.

Mya stood in front of the tall mirror in Gloria's bedroom as they helped her into the delicate dress. It was a perfect fit—after a bit of tucking and pinning.

Her mother came from behind her and slipped a small bedazzled comb into her crown-twist updo. "There. Now you have something blue."

"Mum, does anyone even follow that tradition anymore?"

"Those who want nothing but happiness and bliss in their marriage follow it. Now, your dress is old, your shoes are borrowed. You just need something new…"

"What about my ring? It's new."

"Brilliant. Now you have everything, love."

Mya smiled, willing to indulge her mother with the old tradition. She already had everything she needed, though she loved the idea of eternal happiness with Guy. She knew that nothing—not even the deepest of loves—was without its challenges, but what she and Guy shared was special. No matter what life threw their way, they could withstand anything.

"Mya, honey, are you ready?"

With one last look in the mirror, she nodded. The three of them made it out to the backyard, and her mother and Gloria went to take their seats in the front among her close family and friends.

Mya was grateful the spring weather had decided to behave. The sun was high and the trees were in full bloom. The light breeze served to cool the sun's bright rays, and the blush-pink paper lanterns swayed from their delicate perch along the low-hanging tree branches.

An intense energy surrounded her, and Mya instantly felt her father's presence as she glided down the fuchsia-pink aisle runner. Under the decorated wedding arch stood her husband and the minister. She was unable to tear her eyes away. Guy was impossibly handsome in his black and white tux and with his hair slicked back like that.

A stunned expression flashed on his face before he broke out into a wide grin. When she reached his side, he leaned down and whispered in her ear.

"You're one of a kind, Mya. How did I get so lucky?"

She laughed softly. "Just wait until tonight."

Desire flashed in his eyes and he grinned. "Ready to do this?"

"Oh, yeah."

The minister began the ceremony and Mya found herself lost in the moment as she recited the vows that would lay the foundation of their union.

They had come a long way to get here, but today marked a new beginning for them. No more looking back or wallowing in regrets. Though they had decided to still wait to start a family—a subject they would revisit once the renovations to her father's home were complete and they were settled in.

Besides, they still had much they wanted to accomplish in their professions. She was close to launching her online store and he had only recently returned to work after his recovery. His absence from the department had been felt throughout the station and town, which Mya believed had compelled Mayor Warren to announce Guy's promotion to sheriff of Cedar Bend. Of course, he would always find ways to connect all things positive back to his campaign. But whatever the mayor's purposes, she was happy Guy got to continue doing the job he loved.

Together, they were on a path to start their new lives as husband and wife, and she was excited for their future.

"I hereby pronounce you husband and wife. You may now kiss your bride."

Intense desire burned in Guy's eyes before he swooped her in his arms and kissed her deeply, and without regard to their audience. Mya melted against him as loud cheering resounded around them. But it soon faded in the far distances of her mind as she lost herself in his embrace. He consumed her and she clung to him, her small bouquet of daisies crushed between them.

"Save some for the wedding night!"

Mike's distinct voice rolled through the crowd, and everyone erupted in laughter and more cheering.

Mya giggled. Guy ignored him. Instead, he kissed her again, sealing their love with many promises to come.

❤

Thanks for reading!

If you enjoyed reading this story, please share that with others so they can enjoy it too!

Rate or review this book at your purchasing site or favorite review site (i.e. Amazon, Barnes & Noble, Goodreads, etc.). Honest reviews are always helpful!

Recommend this book to your family, friends, reader groups, or book clubs.

Share this book with others by spreading the word on your favorite social media site.

About the Author

Lena Hart is a Florida native currently living in the Harlem edge of New York City. Though she enjoys reading a variety of romance genres, she mainly writes sensual to steamy romances with a flare of suspense and mystery. When Lena is not busy writing, she's reading, researching, or conferring with her muse. To learn more about Lena and her work, visit LenaHartSite.com.

48234658R00115

Made in the USA
San Bernardino, CA
20 April 2017